C. J. Hughes.

Penguin Books
When the War is Over

Stephen Becker was born in 1927 and was educated
at Harvard, Peking and in Paris. Since 1951 he
has published six novels (including *A Covenant with
Death*, *The Season of the Stranger* and *The Outcasts*),
two works of non-fiction and seven translations
from the French (including *The Last of the Just*).
Married with three children, he lives in Katonah,
New York.

Stephen Becker

When the War is Over

Penguin Books

Penguin Books Ltd, Harmondsworth,
Middlesex, England
Penguin Books Australia Ltd, Ringwood,
Victoria, Australia

First published in the U.S.A. 1969
Published in Great Britain by Hamish Hamilton 1970
Published in Penguin Books 1973

Copyright © Stephen Becker, 1969

Made and printed in Great Britain by
Hunt Barnard Printing Ltd, Aylesbury, Bucks.
Set in Linotype Times

*All the characters in this book are
fictitious and are not intended to represent any
actual person living or dead.*

This book is sold subject to the condition that
it shall not, by way of trade or otherwise, be lent,
re-sold, hired out, or otherwise circulated without
the publisher's prior consent in any form of
binding or cover other than that in which it is
published and without a similar condition
including this condition being imposed on the
subsequent purchaser.

To Keir, Julia and David
with love and thanks

Chapter One

Once upon a time, God save us all, there was an orphan boy called Marius Catto who grew up to be a lieutenant of infantry in the Army of the United States. His platoon was a mixed bag of civilian soldiers who did their job with half the heart, dreaming usually of other matters: fishing or carpentry or a barrel of beer. Otherwise they did what soldiers have always done: followed orders and grumbled. They strolled through leafy woods in a long, lazy rank like so many nobs with fowling pieces, presumed to be rooting out stragglers and guerrillas but in truth squandering as much of the war as possible short of outright treason. Chewing on stalks, dreaming of fat women or great fortunes. Not that it was all palmy: in clearings the sun blistered, and cotton shirts clung. But armies did not wear silk, and they judged that they were all through killing and dying, so when a man complained he was soon rebuked, and reminded of his luck.

Catto sprang from flat country, out west of Chicago where the land lay endless and plain, and he enjoyed these wooded hills, redbud and hickory, and the musical streams that flowed clear and quick between cool, deep pools doubtless full of plump fish; and he liked the colourful birds of the forest, some so small they might have been thought butterflies: finches, and others that he could not name. The earth was hard after a hot summer, and a few leaves and needles had fallen to carpet their way; the men moved quietly. One fine morning Catto was holding down the north end of the string, with Haller at his left and then eight more. It was indeed a fine morning: a bright, perfect September morning full of good smells, forest and field and flower and bird glowing and whispering and crackling and rustling, one of those mornings when the senses were a divine gift and a man hesitated to light his pipe. Catto could see only

Haller; every little while they nodded, like farmers working separate rows.

By the blue grass Catto halted: a sloping meadow, long and open and full of peace, and yonder a smoke-house or corn-crib; from here he could not be sure. Sergeant Haller knelt beside him, grey and wiry, a man who tried not to speak without cause. Catto was grateful for that, in part because it was a tradition that young lieutenants winced when old sergeants preached, in part because all old soldiers were deadly bores. Advice. Irrelevant memories. Mexico. 'Send Routledge to me,' Catto told him. 'Take the others around there to the south. Keep to the woods. I'll go this way with Routledge. Meet us at that far stand of trees, birches, looks like. Don't fire until you see what you're killing.'

Haller nodded and moved off.

Catto blinked away a slight haze, and yawned, and removed his cap to scratch his head of light brown hair, faintly reddish in some lights, which generally itched, being only a trifle less filthy than enlisted men's heads. Then he smoothed his moustache and inspected his Spencer, all in order, sights clean; also the Remington, six chambers full, which had not been fired for months. Most officers preferred the Colt. Catto was partial to the Remington because of that clever notch in the barrel; he could take aim. Ordinarily that made no difference because the enemy was upon him, point-blank, if it came to pistols. But he had killed a man once from a hundred feet with the Remington, at Stones River. He had been trapped until dusk in a ditch, nothing to do but squat hidden and hope. A fellow spotted him and started back for help, and died. Total stranger. A good shot. Then at dusk Catto jumped up and ran like the devil, and in the last light some sharp-shooter sent a ball to crease his bottom. He laughed about it next day. 'You'll be scarred,' the surgeon told him, 'but you won't be showing it off much.' Catto was scarred, in truth: a perfect horizontal furrow. From behind he offered the sign of the cross. ('The true cross,' Phelan said later. Phelan was another surgeon, and a better. 'There will be statues of you in all the churches. You will be the patron saint of the backward.'

'I'm a Protestant,' Catto said. He was naturally ruddy, and talk of religion deepened his blush.

'That's what I mean.' Phelan considered this heretic with affection. 'Where did you come by a name like Marius?' he asked, busy head cocked like a scholar's.

'I don't know. There's no family left. Nobody to explain. We were maybe once Catholic.'

'Everybody was once Catholic,' Phelan mourned. 'In days of yore and back then. Anyway you were lucky. It's a clean scar, and better behind than before.')

He was, he reflected now, still lucky. Lucky to be here, waiting for Routledge, and not in Georgia, where the carnage was wholesale. Or was he? Where should a soldier be? And how should a soldier know?

Routledge approached, quietly enough for a big man who was not interested in war. Catto gave him orders. 'And Routledge.'

'What else, Lieutenant?' Resigned tones.

'Don't fall down, please. Or drop your rifle, or shoot Haller.'

'All right,' Routledge said, crestfallen. He was a Jonah, perversely reliable: every company seemed to harbour, or suffer, one natural catastrophe, outwardly human, normal in all respects save that he could be counted upon absolutely, even under fire when other men dug in, to topple a hot coffee-pot, stumble a tent flap, shoot himself in the foot, tip a sheaf of mail into the campfire or spill soup on a comrade.

Routledge shambled off. The men never bothered with 'sir'. Haller was an old-timer, longer in the army than Catto was on earth. Routledge was forty and had nine children, or so he said. Catto did not care about 'sir'. In his first year as a lieutenant he had lost two swords and been required to buy new ones for parade. Damned silly business, he thought. Secretly he liked ceremony. But at twenty-four he also liked being gruff and democratic.

It was time to rise from his knees and go to work, but he was once more distracted, this time by a shadow, a cloud, whiffling across the face of the sun in a thunderous whisper; he was confused by the windy roar and rustle, by the moment of fear and loss, by a message undelivered, and looked up first in dismay

9

and sorrow and resentment, like a traveller in a cloudburst, and only a second later with a lightning smile of deep pleasure. The sky to the east was black with birds, the sun itself disguised. Thousands of passenger pigeons beat southwards, a flying carpet of them. Catto held his breath. A hundred thousand, might be. They were free. Marvelling up at them he felt pure, the innocence of dawn. He watched in welcome every spring, in godspeed every fall. The birds flew in a vast oval mass, no pairs, no skeins, no wedges, only the great mass of them, and the steady, fading rush across the face of the sun. A dark mass, the blushing breasts obscured, they dimmed the golden morning. Catto flew with them, broke away, soared. Lords of the sky. Catto one of them. He loved the birds and the beasts.

Soon the pigeons were gone, and Catto was staring into the sun. He glanced down into the forest before him, and panicked: he was blind. He saw wheels and hoops and waves of yellow light, the hollows beneath the trees black and purple and writhing, and as he knelt blinking life back into his eyes he thought he saw a boy. The boy was carrying a staff and rising out of the purple shade, all fair and golden-haired, with loops and circles of yellow and red all about him, and then green and blue. For one moment Catto thought he must be going mad, or receiving visions, this golden child in the wilderness like a fairy tale; and then he saw the boy raise the staff and point to him. Catto understood. He sprawled forward on to his belly, but a bit too late, and a red-hot hammer smashed his left shoulder. Damn! Wrong again!

He knew immediately that he had not been killed, not this time, though he felt grey with mortality. There was no pain but he had to fight for breath, as if someone had slammed him against a wall. And then he laughed. He would have a decent rest now, in a bed perhaps, in the city perhaps, and good food, and a fair friend perhaps. But Routledge was up and galloping, so Catto shouted 'Careful!' That was silly. He released the rifle and pushed himself to his knees. Routledge was down again – hit? – and he saw Haller scuttling in a spidery crouch at the far end of the blue meadow. And after him Lowndes and Carlsbach. Catto drew the Remington and waited.

And inspected his shoulder, to pass the time. A little blood, and a hole in the shirt just below the collarbone. Somewhere in there a lead ball. Phelan would find it and extract it. That would hurt. Whisky, and perhaps an opium pill, and Phelan would say, 'That's the hell of it, boy. You lie around drinking good whisky while I work myself to death.'

Catto's left arm hung loose, like a spare part, as if he were a wooden soldier in need of repair; but there was still no pain. He thanked God, deeply, fervently (caring not at all who, or whether, God was), that it was not the spine. Or the private parts.

At halloos and alarms he raised the pistol; but it was Routledge racing back. 'I'm all right,' Catto called out. 'What happened?'

'Got him,' Routledge said, and helped his officer to stand.

'Dead?'

'No.'

'Take the Spencer.'

Haller too came trotting. 'You hurt, Lieutenant?'

'A ball in the shoulder.' He knew an impulse to giggle, and choked it back. 'Who did it?'

'A boy,' Haller said. 'He give up.'

'Any more?'

'Only the one.'

'Maybe. Pickets out?'

Haller's yes was infinitely dry; now Catto tittered. They were into the redbuds and he heard voices.

'That was a good shot. Couple of hundred yards, must be.'

'Hurt much?'

'Just beginning. I'm all right.' Among the trees he saw his men, and a stranger. That one. Cut his throat, I will. Marius the wolf-man.

It was a boy, all right. With white-blond hair. Corporal Godwinson slapped him backhand. Ah, valour.

'Godwinson,' Catto said, 'leave him be. It was me he shot, and I rather a gang of armed men go easy on a child. If you take my meaning.'

The boy was skinny, ragged, his eyes a shiny bright blue. No

11

one spoke for a time. The soldiers rested in the shade of the redbuds and examined their prize. Catto was tired; he glanced down at the pistol, frowned, restored it to its holster. He sniffed: they all smelled bad. Not like the woods or the blue grass, not aromatic, only stinking soldiers. In all wars, he supposed, in all centuries, the same smell. Catto too. 'You smell like livestock,' he said. 'Don't you ever wash? How the Christ can you share a tent?' Godwinson shied, blinking.

The boy was barefoot. Tattered brown trousers, too short, a homespun shirt, collarless. Powder horn, pouch, knife.

'Somebody take that knife. Where's his rifle?'

'Here.'

'God's sake,' Catto said. 'A Kentucky rifle.'

'This is Kentucky,' Carlsbach said.

'Yeh.' He hefted the rifle. Long barrel, fine balance. 'This piece was made before the oldest man here.' On the stock, in small neat curly letters, was incised WILLIAM MARTIN. 'William Martin,' he said. 'That you?'

The boy stood sullen.

'Speak up, boy. Or I'll give you back to that corporal.'

'My father,' the boy said.

'Voice is hardly changed,' Godwinson said.

The boy was tanned, and his face was round, with a modest natural pout to the lower lip. His hair was almost chalk-white, and he had no whiskers, just a fair down on the upper lip, and more on the cheekbones. Maybe one of those albino people, Catto hazarded to himself; but they were said to have pink eyes or ears or some such thing. 'He can shoot, though. What's your name?'

'Thomas Martin,' the boy said.

'Where you from?'

'Over east.'

'Over east. What are you doing here?'

The boy only glared.

So Catto sighed and said, 'Maybe we ought to just shoot him now.'

They all stood staring at the boy.

'You realize you just shot an officer in the United States Army,' Catto said. That too sounded silly.

'I'm a soldier,' the boy said. 'That's what I signed on to do. Made my mark, anyway.'

'Ah. What army you in?'

'Confederate States of America.'

'Where's your uniform?'

'They didn't have none.'

'Not even shoes.' Godwinson snorted. It occurred to Catto, that was the kind of man Godwinson was: the kind of man who knows how to snort.

'They take them young,' Catto said. 'It's all they have left. How old are you?'

'About sixteen,' the boy said. Catto felt old.

'Bottom of the keg,' Carlsbach said.

'Shut up,' Catto told him. 'He shoots better than you.'

'A damn guerrilla,' Godwinson said.

'I ain't a guerrilla,' the boy said, in the firm, admonitory tones of a schoolmaster. 'I signed on with Colonel Jessee.'

'Well. One of Colonel Jessee's riflemen. Where's the colonel now?'

'Don't know. The orders was just to do all the damage we could on our own.'

'That's pretty close to a guerrilla,' Catto said thoughtfully. 'Anyway you did some damage. Give me your horn and pouch.'

'They were my father's.'

'Look, boy, you're a prisoner now. Count yourself lucky we don't just save ourselves the trouble of taking you in.'

'They said you'd kill me,' the boy muttered.

'Well, they were wrong. Give me the horn and pouch.'

The boy handed them over. Catto passed them to Haller. 'Save these for me.'

'What do we do with him?'

'Take him in,' Catto said. 'What else? Tie his hands and let's go. My day's work is done.'

'How is it now?' Haller asked.

'Hurts like hell itself,' said Catto.

'Lie down there,' Phelan said. 'What will they do to him?' Phelan was a tall black Irishman with a face like the man in the moon, round, pocked and pitted and pored by ancient acnes, but lent a scowling force by the belligerent black handlebar moustache. The first surgeon to repair Catto was called Swartz, a pale Dutchman with glasses; that was at Stones River, which they sometimes called Murfreesboro. Then they acquired Phelan, and never saw Swartz again. Phelan talked a good deal. He had hazel eyes, almost yellow with little flecks of brown. They were mild eyes and when you came to know him, sad.

'Court-martial,' Catto said. 'Never mind about him. Relieve my pain.'

'You are only a lieutenant,' Phelan said. 'who has allowed himself to be half killed by a child. I remind you that I am a captain and entitled to exquisite courtesies.' He was cutting away Catto's shirt. 'Threads. Damn threads ground right into you. Easy now. Let me slip it off you.'

'You butcher,' Catto moaned.

'A butcher is all you deserve. What were you doing? Dreaming of women? Fat white bottoms waggling at you?'

'Now there is a subject I would much enjoy discussing someday. The fact is I was watching some pigeons.' Catto was lying nervously on his own cot with blankets heaped up under his head and shoulders, while Phelan snipped. Outside the tent men were laughing and cursing, and he heard a mule clop. 'A big flight of passenger pigeons. They darkened the sun. Pretty.'

'Ah, the poet in you,' Phelan said. The shirt was off. 'All right. Simple. An inch lower and it had your lung. But with the luck of fools it's nothing. Phelan can do this with one hand.'

'It hurts now. At first there was no pain at all.'

'No. You poor lad. You bird-fancier. What you need is warm milk and a few drops of hartshorn. But you will have to settle for a swallow of Saint Kentigern's tears, also called Uncle Mungo's bone solvent. I happen to have about me a quart or more of that sovereign remedy. Spermaceti, spermaceti.'

'Why don't you shut up and just do your job.'

'Well, now.' Phelan beamed, 'part of my job is to comfort the afflicted. Like a priest at home. When asked what was best for the barrenness, he said knightly attentions from a baron. This will leave you a pretty scar.'

'What one more?'

'Right you are. Now when you have finished showing off your hot cross bum you will have to give the ladies a look at the front of you. That is if they can get close enough.'

Catto sucked long at the bottle. 'You are a filthy man and a disgrace to your profession. A barber. When you have finished with that you may give me a trim. Not too short on the sides, please.'

'A wiseacre,' Phelan murmured. 'An infinitely amusing young man. Be careful or I will dock you while I am about it.'

'You could do that by accident,' Catto said. 'You know where the shoulder is, I trust.'

'I hear the boy is only fifteen,' Phelan said. 'I will assume that you have been holding your own with little girls.'

'It was a pretty shot,' Catto drank deep again. 'If I hadn't started to drop he'd have had my heart sure.' The whisky generated a rich heat; fumes rose within him. He drank little in the field and this was blurring him quickly. It was, he imagined, a bit like drowning.

'They're better shots than we are.' Phelan said. 'Hunters. I mind my uncle Fabricius, out fowling when he came upon Howie O'Toole and Mary Spain, at it like great pink pigs – '

'For God's sake. Will you put your mind to the work at hand.'

'Just lie back, now.' Phelan said, soothing, 'and get more of that into you.'

'Where you off to?'

'Why, to fetch my gleaming instruments. And an orderly with hot water. Nothing is too good for officers.'

'This is fine stuff.'

'It will shortly be my turn. Save me about three inches. The sight of blood turns me giddy. Now I must go and heat up my bayonet and cross-cut saw.'

'A great comfort you are. And me dying.'

'*Omnia mors aequat,*' said Phelan.

'What is that? Latin.'

'Latin it is. Death makes all men equal. Anyway it was not I that was ass enough to get shot. It was Lieutenant Marius Catto, our hero and leader.'

'I shot a few myself. This is how I pay for it. Makes it less . . . '

Phelan paused at the flap. 'Less evil, you're trying to say. But the word comes hard.'

'That's it.'

'Well, it's still evil. God grant you don't have to pay for it in some other coin.' Phelan frowned, as if he knew the future.

'It's a necessary evil.' Catto swallowed uneasily. Phelan and God: an unlikely pair. 'Go ask Jacob how necessary. This damn black man's war.' But he had killed and known exultation, and he too feared a revenge; from or by whom or what, he was not sure.

Phelan hooted cheerfully. 'Oh. Now you want me to go to a nigger for instruction in the moral philosophies.'

'Why not? They never kept slaves.' Catto laughed, suffered pain and fell silent. He gurgled more whisky into himself. 'Very good stuff. I must get myself shot every week or so. But I meant it about paying up. That's my lot and not to be complained about. Not too much, anyway. As yours is the stink and pus of your work, or the death of your patients.'

'You talk like a man who has been drinking,' Phelan said. 'Phelan's patients never die. That is the first rule of physic.'

'Glad to hear it,' Catto said slowly. 'I think I will soon sleep for a bit.' He spaced the words deliberately. 'Once we shot about a thousand in half an hour. Over by Pingree Grove. We filled a wagon. It was too many, and we fed the leftovers to the pigs. We killed and killed. As fast as we could load. Three, four with one blast.'

'Be quiet now, and sleep.'

'You're the doctor,' Catto said. 'As a fact, you are two doctors. I see two Phelans. One was more than enough but for my sins I have been shown two. You're the doctors.'

'I am really a veterinarian.' Phelan said, 'and was sent for specially. Keep drinking, lad.'

Five days later Catto was still in pain. So much for Phelan. They heard that Atlanta had fallen. Catto's platoon came by every morning to pay their respects or make fun of him, and Lowndes, who always carried a banjo when he was not fighting, said, 'Maybe it will all be over soon,' and plucked a triumphant chord. Haller sat with Catto outside the tent, talking little. Catto

16

asked him again if he would care to be a lieutenant, and Haller declined again. It was an old argument. 'I've been a sergeant too long,' Haller said. 'And then I'd always have to be polishing a sword and probably trip over it on parade. And then – '

'Go on.'

'Well, you know some of these officers, But I shouldn't be saying that.'

'I know them, all right.' Some of them, God knew why they were officers. An uncle at the courthouse, or elected because they had a horse. Catto had come in a private, by God. Some of them could not be trusted to carry messages if there were any Johnnys on the way. It was not precisely a question of courage. No one knew what that was: a form of insanity, perhaps. With those fellows it was more a question of not getting your nails dirty.

But life yielded up minor blessings: Catto's counterpart in the second platoon had risen above wealth and good looks, and did his job without fuss or fribble. Lieutenant Silliman's father was a rich miller and had considered running for Congress; Lieutenant Silliman was nevertheless a virtuous man (barring an icy, savagely efficient passion for poker) and an estimable soldier. 'I'm sorry you hurt,' he said. 'Do you need anything? I have some extra sugar. And coffee.'

'That is excessively kind of you,' Catto intoned, and Silliman coloured immediately. 'What do you want to be such a gentleman for? Why don't you tell me what a fool I was to be shot like that?'

'Anybody can get himself shot.'

'But first lieutenants aren't supposed to. Second lieutenants, yes, you, but not a serious professional like me. And now you'll have extra work because I'm out of it.'

'I don't mind that. And I feel sure that the killing is almost over, I really do.'

'You feel sure. Ned, you are either the damnedest fool in the whole world or the hope of the future, which is unlikely.' Catto considered this young fellow gravely. Tall. Curly blond hair. White teeth. Neat and balanced features. Stank rarely. Clean-shaven. In garrison he would be kind to his orderly. He would call old men 'sir' and offer an arm to old ladies. 'And you come over here to tell me you're sorry I hurt.'

'What? What does that mean?'

'Never mind. Coffee is a good idea. But we'll drink mine.'

'All right.' Silliman sprang to work. In time of peace he would wear ruffled shirts. 'And you can tell me about the wound. Did it hurt when he dug for the ball?'

Phelan had mined a small chip of collarbone from Catto's flesh and worried that there might be others. Catto could not move in any comfort so spent most of his day sitting back against a tree, with his shirt off. The sun was pleasant and there were those little birds. Men moved about as if they had things to do, but you could tell from their faces and their slouch that it was aimless motion. The cooks kept busy. Jacob worked hard. Jacob was a freed slave. He was their carpenter, porter, skinner, runner, latrine orderly, trash collector and second cook. He earned his found and two dollars a week in silver. Catto did not know what he did with the money. Perhaps buried it. Jacob ate a lot and cadged tobacco for his cherry-wood pipe, and wore cast-offs. He was an average-sized man, pretty strong. He liked that pipe. It was hardly ever out of his mouth except when he was feeding his face. He was another quiet one. Always looking at his feet.

So Catto sat and watched wise, indifferent mules shuffle past. Either the regiment had removed itself from the war or Thomas Martin was the last guerrilla: patrols went out half asleep and returned half asleep. You would not have thought they were at war except for the number of slovenly malcontents wearing uniforms. Thieves and liars who never washed. Perhaps they had existed in time of peace too, but when, as a boy, Catto had dreamed of the army he had imagined men who bore themselves with pride and knew what they were about. This mob was always on the look-out for entertainment. Cards and tall stories and sometimes a cock fight, two bedraggled roosters each more frightened than the other. If the men had been cavalry they would have laid out a race track. Haller complained about them once, long and loud, and then no more; doubtless he had been in the trade long enough to accept anything.

18

Phelan came by to renew dressings, and to adjust the sling, fussing like a grandmother and gossiping even worse. Half the time Catto could not understand this nervous, prancy Irish high-stepper with rolling eyes, who gabbled on and on, throwing in his bits of the Bible and Shakespeare and God knew what. Being inactive and unemployed Catto noticed it more. 'It is perhaps a drop of Welsh blood,' Phelan said. 'My own people are more solemn and judicious.'

'Yeh. The Ninetieth Illinois.'

'Now, now,' Phelan said. The 90th Illinois was an Irish regiment and known for babble. It was said that they jabbered the Johnnys into surrender: two days across the lines from them and you gave up just for a bit of silence. One of them was supposed to have reported the death of their colonel, and when this was questioned he said, 'Indade he is kilt; I heard him say so wid his own mouth.' Phelan was sensitive about this. He was sensitive about many things. When his eyes stopped rolling and flashing they grew melancholy. Somewhere in him was a great bitterness. Perhaps it had to do with doctoring. Or with being so educated. Schooling was some years behind Catto. Phelan had revealed once that he studied at the Cooper Union in New York before learning medicine, and with the priests before that. 'I don't like this,' he said now, and undid the dressing. 'This is not as clean as I would want.'

'I don't like it either. It hurts.'

'It is mortified somewhat.'

'Then do something about it. What are you paid for?'

'Paid! I have not been paid since the month of June. They keep the money in a barrel in Cincinnati. By the way, they say Atlanta is all burned down.'

'Give me a cigar.'

Phelan struck a pine match for him.

'Where do you get those?'

'A good doctor has his little oddments,' Phelan said. 'These are dangerous. They fly apart and burn holes in your shirt. Also do not breathe the phosphorus. Anyway, you have fine weather for your convalescence.'

That was true. The days were beautiful, and the finches were company. In the light breezes of late summer the trees seemed to breathe.

'And you are not out there being shot full of holes.'

'One is enough.'

'Yes. And a nasty one. You must pray.'

'Just cover it up again,' Catto said. 'I don't like the look of it, and when it's open like that I can't help squinting at it.'

'Yes.' Phelan brooded. 'We are all full of life and juices, and then something pops or splits or swells up, and we are dead in a day. I wonder if Adam and Eve ever cut themselves. Were there thorns in Eden. Did he ever choke on a pomegranate seed, and cough it up with a spot of blood. Did she moan with the gripes when the courses were upon her. Aquinas is obscure on the question.'

'For God's sake.'

'There. You'll live to fight another day. You have my promise.'

'Thanks. What about this mortification? Is it serious?'

'I hope not,' Phelan said. 'It is just some dead flesh and a small angriness. Threads and bone chips. We'll give it a few days more and see what happens. Keep the sling on. If you die I will recommend you for promotion.'

'But I don't want to be a captain,' Catto said. 'Captains talk too much.'

Young and restless, Catto wandered, and chaffed the cooks, and leaned on the fence at the corral to watch the mules. He went to the river every day and washed his feet, which was not easy with one hand. He ate his S.B. and black beans and day-dreamed of steaks and pigeon pie. S.B. was what they all called sowbelly. He would have enjoyed something to read, but there was not much. Some almanacs full of bad jokes and grotesque women. A Bible. He played cards one night, also not easy with one hand, though he quit richer. Colonel Bardsley sent for him and said, 'Lieutenant Catto. Sit down there. Rest easy. How does it feel?'

'Not good,' he said. 'I'm weak at times.'

'Phelan will have you right. I want to know about this boy.'

'All I know is in my report.'

'Yes. What do you make of this story about Colonel Jessee?'

'It could be true. All the boy had to do was raise his right hand and be sworn in.' Catto smiled wearily. 'Anyway, we're all guerrillas here. That's how we licked the British.'

'Yes.' The colonel was one of those stocky red men, like a big feed-and-grain dealer. Seemed almost to smell of mash. A professional soldier, though. Bald. Reddish chin-whiskers. 'Well. You'll have to testify.'

'Court-martial?'

'Yes.'

'Seems silly,' Catto murmured. 'If you don't mind my saying so. The boy's only sixteen. You can't try him like a man. And it was me he shot, and I'm not upset.'

The colonel smiled. 'In the classic words of the bard,' he said, 'you showed your ass that time.'

'Yes sir. I feel embarrassed, but I have nothing against the boy.'

'Well, it's only a formality. Nobody's going to hurt the lad.'

'That's fine. When's the trial?'

'Not until we get back. I expect that will be soon.'

'Very good.'

'Take care of that shoulder,' the colonel said. 'We'll see if we can get you another bar to sew on top of it. Captain Catto. Sounds good.'

'Thank you, sir.' That was twice it had come up. Perhaps an omen. It would mean more money.

Meanwhile he went on wandering. They were at half strength and it was not much of a bivouac. Rubbish lay neglected, scraps of paper and cigar butts, old tobacco sacks and spills, rags, empty paper cartridge cases, splinters of wooden crates, condensed-milk cans. If Catto had been their colonel he would have ordered a general policing. He might have been a colonel once. At twenty-three. Over black troops. The Union freed them but could not persuade officers to lead them. Catto had declined.

Probably it was the sight of Jacob that made him think about the colonelcy, with a light nip of regret. Jacob was at the corral, leaning on the bars with his pipe stuck in his mouth.

Catto went the other way, and found Haller, and told him to see that the platoon kept its own area clean.

But a few days more and he could not abide the smell of his wound, and Phelan rubbed mint into the dressings. 'It's not good,' the surgeon said. 'Now I don't like it at all.'

'I'm hot. Silliman is worried.'

'Silliman worries about the Ten Commandments. Ignore him. But you have dead flesh there that is not sloughing. Some of it is inside and I don't want to cut that deep but something must be done about the mortification.'

They were still outside Catto's small tent at dusk. Phelan smoked and Catto chewed. With only one free hand chewing was easier than waving a cigar about. Weeks before there had been a myriad of bats at dusk, tiny swift-shuttling shadows to weave a new night, but now there were none; the presence of men had driven them off. Men. Huge land-bound creatures with no grace. There was not much grace to chewing tobacco either, but it was a pastime. Though even spitting, the turn of the head and the stretch of the neck, caused Catto pain. And he was sleeping badly: unwearied, galled.

'Yes,' Phelan said, and then, pensively, 'I am going to clap a small poultice on you, full of medicine. It will feel creepy and crawly but don't mind that. It is an old remedy and the best thing.'

'What kind of medicine?'

'The kind every veterinarian is familiar with,' Phelan said, cheerful again. 'I won't tell you now. Later.'

Catto groaned. 'An experiment. It will be manure, or mud made with horse piss.'

'No. Neither. I promise you.'

Half an hour and he was back with dressings and a small box. He laid bare the wound and grimaced. 'Ah, my poor boy. Should have joined the navy.'

'That's a joke too,' Catto said. 'I joined the army because I like horses, and have been in the infantry from the first day. Careful. That hurts.'

'Courage,' Phelan said, in the French way. 'Just removing

22

some loose garbage.' With his back to Catto in the lantern light he prepared his mysterous poultice, and then he turned to press it against Catto's shoulder. It was roundish like a small breast, and in the hollow of it was his witches' brew. 'Hold that tight now while I tie it on. Tight now. Under the arm,' he crooned, 'and across the back, and around the neck, and there. Good. It must be kept tight. Remember. Sleep on your back. Don't cheat about the sling.'

'You ass,' Catto said. 'Of course on my back. Do you think I've been sleeping on the wound? It does feel creepy and crawly.'

'It will do the job,' Phelan said. 'And now I think a nip would help, and I have a piece of gossip to cheer you.' He pulled a flask from his pocket and passed it to Catto. Uncle Mungo's whatever. Catto's body seemed to blot it up; it was warm and jolly. With the flask Phelan sketched a salute, and drank.

'Cheer me,' Catto said.

'Cincinnati, my boy. Early next week. The whole regiment. Garrison duty. and with luck we will not see a field or a forest again until this war is over.'

'Ah.'

'Ah. indeed. Payday. Some juicy beef.'

'Juicy – '

'I thought that might occur to you. Ah to be a lusty cock of twenty-five again.'

'Twenty-four.'

'Twenty-four. Ten years between us.' Phelan now sucked long at his flask. and passed it blindly back. and Catto wondered what those sad eyes saw. 'My God,' Phelan said as if answering, 'I would like to step inside a real church again and smell incense. I am an old man of thirty-four and I miss the Mass as much as I miss the lass . . . I've embarrassed you.'

'Only that you talk about them in the same breath.'

'Not only that.'

'I never had a Catholic friend before. You people seem to believe so much harder.' Catto was uneasy again. If only he had been sure of anything. But his uncertainties left him naked.

'Well, we don't talk back,' Phelan said, and then more briskly,

'However. The subject at hand is Cincinnati, and not only Cincinnati, but a new commanding general for the department. One to whom the, ah, masculine necessities and prerogatives are of the first importance.'

This was news. 'Who's that?'

'Fighting Joe Hooker himself.'

Catto groaned.

'Now, now,' Phelan said. 'You are wrong to bleat so. That's the fellow the glass of whisky is named after, not to mention the scarlet woman. A distinction you and I cannot claim, or even better men. Have we a class of ladies known as Shakespeares? Or a tot of liquor called a Byron? No. But hookers we have, and thank God for both sorts.'

Catto whimpered his pleasure. 'It's been a while. Make me well, doctor. Make me well soon.'

'For I fain wad lie doon.' Phelan laughed and then said primly, 'Something must be done about your soul.'

'When the war is over.'

'Good enough.' Phelan blessed him in a flutter of fingers. 'There is precedent for the request. When the war is over you will look to your soul.'

'Righty-oh,' said Catto. 'Now that flask, please.'

In a day or two the fever did subside, and Catto felt a bit more bright-eyed and hairy-chested. The bivouac was livelier, with good news circulating, and the usual speculations and embellishments. Even Godwinson smiled with his thin lips and icy eyes. But when he said, 'How's the shoulder, Lieutenant?' Catto wondered if the man's smile was for the good news or at a foolish man who had let himself be shot by a child. Godwinson did that to you. He said 'Nice day' and you wondered what he meant. He should have been a scout, alone. Even in time of peace he was at war. Carlsbach and Lowndes and the others were calmer, more ordinary; you could see them marching home to a wife and a cow, grateful for a whole skin and the war forgotten in a week, to be remembered in maybe twenty years when it would make a good story. But not Godwinson. Anyway Catto said, 'Better today, thanks,' and they traded talk about Cincinnati. Then Godwinson said, 'You know, they're just letting that kid run around loose.'

'The boy?'

'Yeh. He don't seem to mind at all. Eats his head off.' Godwinson's eyes were empty. He was waiting judiciously.

'Whose orders?'

'The colonel's.'

'Then I guess it's all right,' Catto said with a hint of cold reproach. 'They parole Johnnys and send them home, you know.'

'The kid's a guerrilla.'

'Oh, come on, Godwinson. The kid's a kid.'

Godwinson shrugged, and let be: 'You wouldn't talk that way if you were dead.'

The corral was a makeshift of saplings beside a disused barn. Theirs was strictly light infantry; even lieutenants went on foot. Captains and more exalted orders rode. Phelan commanded a couple of wagons, for his supplies and the badly wounded or very sick. Except for Catto his practice was now confined to disorders of the bowels. Thank God. Catto could remember pest camps worse than prisons, with typhus and smallpox wedged together and not much to be done for anyone. Spotted fever killed quite a few. They all worried about ticks. In 1862 a friend of his had survived three months in a pest camp and come out bald. Catto wondered if the man had ever grown another crop.

The old barn was well built, a cool and musty place. They had shut the boy in there under guard for a day or two and then, with the sensible indifference that alone makes army life bearable, let him out and told him to behave himself. He should have run for it. Later on it was easy to see that. But he hung about, cheerful and willing, and gave Jacob a hand with the mules. Sergeant Hillis – a private, but the horse-sergeant was always a private, and was always called sergeant – was an old hostler and handled the horses himself, jealously. They were handsome animals. All they had to do was to carry officers here and there; they were quick and long-boned, sleek, well fed now in September and October. Catto would not have bet much on

25

their endurance, but they had little need of it. They lived a good life. Let them geld you and brand USA on your rump, and let some fool sit on you, and your troubles were over.

When Catto was tired of the company street he drifted out to the corral and found a soft patch of grass under a nearby tree, and watched the horses for a while, or dozed. Hillis tolerated him. What Hillis despised was the experts who came gaggling around and showed off for one another. Fetlocks and pasterns. Or tried to talk him into setting up a race. He asked the colonel once to declare the corral out of bounds, which proved impossible. Hillis never minded Catto, though. Catto just sat, letting his equine affinities unfold and expand. Horses were old friends; conversation was unnecessary.

Catto was half asleep one afternoon, the sunlight warm, motherly, dappling through the chestnut leaves, when Jacob and the boy came walking along and leaned on the fence.

'That one,' Jacob said. 'That one there long in the hind leg.'

'He's bigger than the others,' the boy said. 'And fatter.'

'And stronger.'

'Maybe.'

'But that sergeant won't let him race.' Jacob said, and laughed quietly. 'He's a hard man.'

'He's all right.' Thomas Martin said. 'He don't look funny at me like the others. He don't act like a soldier at all, really.'

'That's true,' Jacob said. 'He call me Jacob.'

'What's everybody else call you?'

'Darky,' Jacob said, 'or nigger, or coon, but not Jacob. One major called me black'moor once. Never heard that before.'

'Well, you're free.'

Jacob laughed again. 'That's right. And I like it. Silver dollars. All the same.'

'All the same what?'

'When I was a slave in Tennessee,' Jacob said, 'everybody call me Jacob.'

The boy shrugged. 'Don't matter much what they call you. Long as you get paid. You get beaten much before?'

'No,' Jacob said. 'I tell you the difference between slave and free.'

The boy smiled. 'All right. Tell me. We never had a slave.'

'In Tennessee was forty men working for one man. Here, is one man working for forty men.'

They both giggled, and then overflowed, cascading splashes of hawhawhaw, hawhawhaw. Catto grinned. This was, he felt, instructive, and he enjoyed the warm, soft, chewy southern voices.

After a time Jacob said, 'They don't like me. Some of these here soldiers never see a nigger till the war. They scared. They scared of Jacob,' and he laughed again.

'They ain't scared of me,' the boy said ruefully.

They talked more about the horses.

'Hey,' Catto said. 'How you, boy?' He had frightened them, and was sorry.

'Didn't see you, Lieutenant.'

'Hello, Jacob.'

'Yessa,' Jacob said.

The boy's face relaxed into curiosity. He was wary but there was a baby's innocence to him. It kept breaking through. 'How you feeling, Lieutenant?'

'Some better.' Catto said. 'I see they let you loose.'

The boy nodded, and tried a shy smile. 'I reckon they figure I've done all the harm I'm going to.'

So Catto answered his smile: 'Probably. No hard feelings.'

'Well, that's good,' the boy said. 'I never shot a man before.' And after a moment, 'I don't feel right about it.'

'C'est la guerre.'

'What's that mean?'

'That's war. I don't suppose anybody feels right about it.'

'Is that so,' the boy said. 'You ever shoot anybody?'

'Yeh. Killed some. I don't expect I'll ever feel right about it.' And yet. And yet.

'Then there's lots going to feel bad for a long time,' the boy said. 'You should have left us alone.'

'I won't argue politics with you. Main thing is to stay alive and not get crippled up.'

'Yeh,' the boy said. 'I reckon you're about to win this war anyway.'

'Looks like.' Catto said. 'That's one way to end it.' He rose, a bit stiff here and there. The boy and Jacob moved together.

'Thomas Martin,' said Catto. 'Well, that's a name I'll remember. Last fellow shot me, I never had time to get his name.'

'Well, I wish I hadn't,' Thomas Martin said.

'So do I,' said Catto, but he was laughing, and soon the boy laughed too, and then Catto left them, smacking the boy a friendly punch on the arm as he passed by. The boy was all right. He looked straight at you. When he grew up and got a little strength to his nose, a little character around the eyes, he would make a lot of trouble for a lot of girls. For a moment Catto might have been his father.

Soon the bivouac as a whole began to show signs of humanity and intelligence. The certainty of departure – which now amounted almost to the certainty of peaceful retirement – gave the men a new grace, a new calm. Catto came upon them sewing, or boiling off lice, or cutting one another's hair. Thomas Martin was issued new clothes. He betrayed no discomfort in Union blue. The men ragged him about turning coat, and he smiled his bright smile. Shooter and shot met in the company street, and the boy burlesqued a scowl and said, 'I never did get to wear grey.'

'You look just fine in blue,' Catto said. 'Like a soldier.' That cheered the boy. The weather held good and cheered them all. They were gliding into October and nights were cooler, but the days were warm, dry, sunny, full of life, as if this year would see no bleak decline, no southering swarms of geese, no bare, black, leafless forests, no seas of snow. Catto's first year or two were all rain, it seemed now. The Johnnys were only the second enemy. He had marched through weeks and months of rain, counties and states of rain; he fought in rain and slept in mud, and weapons fouled overnight. Why did he remember the rain and forget the rest? They had chanted:

> Now I lay me down to sleep
> In mud that's many fathoms deep;
> If I'm not here when you awake,
> Just hunt me up with an oyster rake.

Catto had never seen an oyster. He had eaten freshwater clams and liked them.

Well, now he was dry and now he was safe, and so were they all. Not a man there had honestly believed he would survive the war, and now not a man thought otherwise. They smiled without knowing why. Forgot to complain about the food. Teased the boy about women until he loured in confusion; that was their own impatience. Smug, they were, and seemed fatter. Catto laughed aloud, thinking that they were like a company of women with child: slow of gesture, pleasant of mouth, complacent of eye.

His shoulder gave him no pain; it was stiff, but the fever was gone and he was left sleepy. When the colonel announced that they would break camp next morning, Catto asked Phelan to come and remove the wrappings. Phelan bragged a bit, and after the noon meal they went back to Catto's tent, and Phelan removed the sling and had Catto straighten the arm, and then he cut through the dressing and very carefully lifted off his enigmatical mound of ox blood or sassafras or whatever it was.

The wound was clean and smoothly healed, with a pretty dimple. 'Good work,' Catto told him. 'You're hired. I suppose you want a greenback to hang on the wall.'

'It was a hard case,' Phelan said. 'The patient was not robust, and was born simple.'

'All right. Now. What was that garbage you used for medicine? That stuff inside the bandage?'

'Oh that. Merely man's best friend. Nature's remedy. God's cure for the ills of the flesh.'

'Poetry. What was it?'

'I'll show you,' Phelan said, and there was that odd, melancholy look to him, like a conjurer pitying his yokel audience because only he knows that his tricks are really magic, and the sly questions from the know-it-alls mere foolishness. He held forth the dressing, to let Catto look.

In the little hollow were four fat white maggots.

Chapter Two

Catto was offended by the court-martial. What had been a duel, lost honourably and without resentment, became a charade, himself an inept harlequin, a clown in blue. His first notice of it was a letter, instructing him to appear before the court, when and where (the how he knew: full uniform, sword; and the why he supposed he knew, from an occasional twinge in his shoulder). The letter galled him, not by its message but by its presumption, its bland reduction of Catto himself to a minor comic character tripping on doorsills, codpiece flapping, eyes rolling whitely. He had heard no gossip, no whisper, and had hoped that the army, his army, would have the good sense to be manly, reasonable, chary of such trivia, perhaps spanking the boy and sending him along home. More than that: it did not seem right to him that the boy be accused, much less locked up, marched about under guard, flung into the maw of justice, records, history, without Catto's consent. All that for an honest misdemeanour when even Haller, his best soldier, was a free felon, a thief of beef, of bags of beans and sacks of sugar sold or swapped for cash or tobacco. 'This I do not like,' he grumbled, waving the letter.

'The Confederacy in gratitude has offered you a decoration,' Phelan said.

'Shut up. These sons of bitches are going to court-martial the boy. I have to testify.'

'Court-martial!' Silliman was shocked rigid.

'Then lie,' Phelan blathered. 'Tell them you shot yourself in the hope of an early return to your job at the bank. It would be less humiliating.'

'You are a funny fellow and all that. But I don't like it. What can they do to the boy? Hang him? Throw him into jail? No.

So why do they have to bother? It is a kind of machinery for its own sake. I have learned only one thing in the army, really.' He stood up, and paced. Phelan had a Sibley tent to himself, like a grand, luxurious tepee, one of the last, you hardly saw them now, his infirmary, medications and instruments heaped and scattered on small tables, and three cots for his patients, and a stove, and two large chests, and two wooden armchairs, salvaged or commandeered.

'Not to keep your head down, that's sure.'

'No.' Catto smiled; he looked back upon his second wound with a gentle affection. 'Or yes. In the field, no, but in Cincinnati, yes. Keep your head down and never look authority in the eye, or it will notice you and strike up a conversation. Haller knows that and would rather be a sergeant than a lieutenant. And these niggers we have around now. Nobody can tell them apart and they are safe that way. So the Martin boy looked somebody in the eye and now he is noticed and they are about to strike up a conversation. Unnecessary and worrisome.'

'Garrison life disagrees with you,' Phelan said. 'It was you he looked in the eye, just before he pulled the trigger. The hell, man, the army has a certain honour and dignity, and cannot allow children to snipe freely at its officers.'

'Then they ought to ask me before they go complicating matters.'

'You miss the point. He wasn't shooting at you. He was shooting at a uniform.'

'And? He was on the other side.'

'So he was.' Phelan prinked, smoothing both wings of his belligerent moustache. 'But I wish he had worn, or had about him, some article of regular Johnny equipment.'

'Me too,' Catto said. He gloomed, then cheered. 'Oh well. I'll speak up for him.'

'Do that,' Phelan said. 'Tell them you were running away at the time. It's unsporting to shoot a sitting lieutenant. One may, however, take them on the rise.'

'I think I'll tell them,' Catto said tentatively, 'that I was about to shoot the boy myself.'

'No. Don't lie. Whatever you do don't lie. Because if you lie and he tells the truth then they will call him the liar. Whatever the stories. You understand?'

'That's right. Fair enough: no lies.'

'Good. Let's eat.'

'Yours to command. By the bye, I want to get Routledge out of the army. He's too old for this, and more trouble than use. Can you help?'

'There you go again,' said Phelan, 'looking authority in the eye. I will not lie for Routledge. But I know a pretty young thing who could give him the pox.'

'God Almighty,' Catto said. 'Surgeons.'

Silliman was scarlet.

Catto was also offended by Cincinnati, by a populous garrison, by company streets, by reeking latrines, by idle men. He had not become a soldier to suffer stinks, to bestow groceries, to rebuke country boys for relieving themselves on public thoroughfares, to inspect for lice and order boilings. Even bayonets had retired, to become furniture, jabbed deep into earth or wood, a candle wedged within the ring: soldiers' lamps. 'They were never any use,' Phelan said. 'Maybe one wound in two hundred was a bayonet wound. You are all cowards.'

'Damn right,' Catto said. 'A line of them coming at you, and it takes you fifteen seconds to load. If you miss, you do not loiter. You run away.'

'Ah, yes, of course.' Phelan's brows bounced; his eyes brightened, jolly. 'It reminds me of an old story.'

Catto waited respectfully.

'A famous battle,' Phelan went on, 'between the English and the French, long since. They were all in those lunatic lines of battle that no one had the sense to improve upon, everybody standing up straight right next to everybody else, and the English tipped their hats, or their gold bonnets or whatever, and said, "Gentlemen of the French guard, please fire first." '

'Good God. That's more manners than I have.'

'That's what most people say. But it was not manners at all. Whoever fired first was helpless for half a minute afterwards, what with reloading, and blinking their eyes, and wiping their noses, and coughing out the smoke, and the young ones changing their trousers. The English were being sly.'

'And the French fell for it, and the English whipped them.'

'Not at all. Practically anybody is smarter than an Englishman. The French declined the honour.'

'And massacred the English.'

'Wrong again.' Phelan was visibly delighted with himself. 'The English fired first, and blew the French to pieces. Cut them to shreds.'

Catto guffawed.

'You laugh. But the French won the battle,' Phelan said. sternly. 'That is called justice.'

'I'm glad I missed it,' Catto said. 'It sounds worse than bayonets, which I am also glad I missed.'

'Afraid of cold steel,' Phelan scoffed. 'Not like the Irish guards at Waterloo.'

'Never mind Waterloo. And never mind your *omnis morris equus* either.'

'The truth is they were Scots,' Phelan said sadly. 'The colonel and I would like more sulphate of iron in the sinks. You want the job?'

'Yes. And anything else you find. I have to keep the men busy.'

'That's the problem now.'

'They're gambling.'

'They'll be brangling in a month.'

For a time his men had been no trouble. ('My men': now and then he called them that, smiling down a childish pride. But they were less than a gallant band, his scrubby fraternity of tatterdemalion kerns.) They cheered and whistled at their log barracks, shouted 'Hey cookie, breakfast tonight' at the fat, weary master of pot and pan, gazed upon the officers' cabins as if upon Rome, and fell into reverent silence before the freshly turned, cleanly patterned grid of sinks, with shovels evenly spaced, upright, permanent as crosses in a graveyard. (Tubby, unwashed Private Franklin had already eased himself against a log wall and been cursed out by Catto, who called him, among other exquisite epithets, a pig's bladder, causing Haller to cackle aloud. Franklin was thenceforth known as Piggy.)

Cincinnati itself was still some way off, but the dust of the roads, the passage of horses, of mule-drawn wagons, of buckboards bearing women and children, all betrayed peace and civilization. The men settled in, and sexless marriages were dissolved; any two who shared a dog tent were called the old man and the woman ('Who's your wife?' was a common question, and not a joke), but now they all slept in two rows of ten or a dozen, an aisle between. A pot-bellied stove presided at one end of the barracks so that a sooty pipe could run the length of the building, saving fuel, lavishing heat; each man in turn sat up for two hours, watching in the night and adding billets. City life. They boiled water in the cook-pots and washed clothes, blankets, kerchiefs, everything but themselves, until Catto issued soap and orders. 'Feet,' he said. 'If nothing else, your cruddy feet. Draw socks this afternoon. I catch you without them, you stand on a barrel all day.'

And then Catto became a foreman, an alderman: the men were a sulking mass of inept municipal employees. Garbagemen, carpenters, ditch-diggers, tailors, grocers, courthouse loiterers, road-menders, tinkers, cooks, petty grafters, wheelwrights – anything but soldiers. Traders and hagglers: half of them had lost, or discarded, or swapped their blankets and overcoats, traded off Canton flannel drawers for coffee; they were allowed forty-two dollars a year for clothes but relied on generous quartermasters. They used postage stamps and scrip for money, and came to Catto when the rain had pulped their life's savings. In three weeks they turned sullen. After almost three years Catto was learning what it meant to be a soldier. 'Only because the war is over. Over for us, and everybody knows it, and they want to go home.'

'Keep them in line,' the colonel said. 'General Hooker is a tough one, and will come down on them hard. Make sure they know that. Hooker has the whole department on his hands and does not want to be distracted by us wee folk.'

'I don't suppose you could have me transferred.'

'No.'

And he lived a mile from the stables now; even that diversion was denied him. He smiled still, as when a recruit joined them and the men sent him to draw an umbrella, and the young fellow trotted off eagerly; but his smiles were brief and testy. 'New men!' he said to Haller. 'We need to get rid of the old ones.'

'Yeh. They'll all be sick soon. Get rid of a few that way.'

'Spoken like a sergeant,' Catto said. 'I'd rather die like Garesche.'

'Garesche?' Haller was startled. 'That priest in Cincinnati? The chaplain?'

'No, hell, no, that's his brother. The dead one was an officer at Murfreesboro. The time I talked with Rosecrans. You mean I never told you that?'

'No.' Haller half smiled. 'You going to draw a long bow on me?'

'God's truth,' Catto said. 'I was scouting at Stones River and chasing back to headquarters, on foot, when Rosecrans come pounding up on that crazy-legged bay he liked, and all his staff galloping behind, and he was bright red. I mean crimson. His uniform was soaked and his hat was dripping. 'General!' I called out. 'You hurt?' And he shouted, 'Get on with it, boy. It's Garesche's blood,' and he galloped off. They told me later that he and Garesche were riding along side by side and a cannonball sheared off Garesche's head. Clean off. One second Lieutenant-Colonel Julius Garesche, the general's chief of staff, next second the headless horseman spraying blood like a geyser. Burst like a boil. I was damn glad to be on foot and low to the ground.'

'Wouldn't have helped. I knew a man had both legs crushed by a cannonball. He was just standing there in the sunshine wondering which way to run. Hell of a thing.'

'Yeh. I went back for an ambulance wagon one time and passed a stack of arms and legs big as a haycock, where they were amputating. Jesus. That had a stink to it.'

'War stinks.'

'War stinks is right. Well, that's our trade. Now I have to go and get that boy out of trouble. Rather be fighting any day. You ever been court-martialed?'

'Nope. I'm what they call a shrewd old soldier.'

Catto smiled. 'That's what I hope to be some day. We got bold soldiers and we got old soldiers. But we got no old bold soldiers.'

Haller, who had heard everything before, nodded politely.

'Well, I better not be late,' Catto said. 'Wish me luck.'

'It's the boy that needs it.'

Catto bumbled huffily up the white wooden steps, chopped a surly salute at the athletic young sentry, and after brief palaver was ushered to an anteroom, a sun parlour, bare and chill and not much warmed by the presence of Corporal Godwinson and Private Poo Padgett. 'Stand up at least,' he said. They did so, Godwinson smiling slightly, and Catto said, 'For God's sake, sit down.' Padgett was one of those boys of nineteen or so, five feet nine or ten, medium-dark, fine teeth, one pimple, never sick a day since the mumps, who escorted their girl friends home from church. Godwinson was Godwinson, and sat calm, not fidgeting, invulnerable. Catto too sat down, exhaled like a blown horse, and stared in panic at his polished boots. 'Greatcoat time,' he said.

They sat in silence. In the nervous interval Catto grew conscious of his body. Not its shape or colour or health, simply its corporeality. The weight of his hams on the hard chair; muscles of the thigh and calf that seemed to flex and extend now of their own will, invisibly and irresistibly; the gentle rise and fall of his chest, the air streaming through his nostrils, the light, persistent beat of his blood. And I will sit there with a rumbling stomach. Or twitch, or break wind, or the colonel will admonish me to wipe my nose. Well. Just keep my hands still and think pure thoughts, and mind my language, and come down hard on any devils inside me.

He stood to attention, once more a wooden soldier. One colonel, one major, one captain, one lieutenant and one sergeant ignored him. The colonel was a black beard, the major sideburns, the captain a red beard, the lieutenant moustachioed, also the sergeant. Blue eyes, brown eyes, snake's eyes, cow's eyes. To Catto's left another sergeant, at ease, armed. Catto was conscious of Thomas Martin, of whispers, lawyer-soldiers, men with pens, and he ached for the field, for a tent beside a stream and a plump bird to roast.

Then he was swearing to something, and was seated, and saw the boy, held down an impulse to wave, and was asked to recite, confining himself to fact and observation. He did so, not omitting the pigeons but passing over the loops and circles of red and yellow light.

'And do you recall what was said by the prisoner upon his capture?'

Catto recalled.

'And what was found upon the prisoner?'

Catto catalogued.

'Not one article of rebel issue?'

Not one.

'And afterwards?'

'We took him back,' Catto said. 'He made no trouble. He was locked in a barn for a day or two but then paroled. Temporarily. He helped out around the bivouac.'

'That's irregular.' The sergeant had spoken. Ah, damn sergeants!

'It's an irregular war. Let me tell you a story. I heard this from a friend in Georgia.' Ten eyes, astonished: do go on. 'There was this Dutchman in the Twenty-sixth Illinois, and a Johnny wanted to quit and come over. So the Dutchman said, "All right, all right, come on," and the Johnny came over, and the Dutchman had been filling canteens at a spring, so he told the Johnny to load up with them and come along, and he never bothered to take away the Johnny's rifle and all that. So the two of them came in, and there was the colonel, and the Dutchman says, "Colonel, here is a prisoner that has come over." And the colonel looked at them and said, "For God's sake, Dutchman, which one is the prisoner?" '

Silence.

Catto stewed in annoyance and embarrassment. 'What I mean is it's that kind of war, you see. In the lines I've traded Johnny salt for fresh vegetables. I got a jug of whisky once for cigars.'

Private Catto, he thought. They ripped away his buttons and

broke his sword. Drums. He shuffled down the long dusty company street. The pariah dog Catto. His own men turned away. Women spat.

'Lieutenant Catto,' the colonel said, 'you are not on trial here – not yet, at any rate,' and five fighting men tittered, 'and the import of your humorous story is not lost upon us. But as the sergeant said, releasing the prisoner was irregular.'

'But we've sent rebel officers home by the dozen,' Catto objected.

'Ah yes,' the colonel said, amiable, benign. 'Officers.'

Catto risked a glance at the sergeant, whose eyes were downcast. 'Yes, sir,' Catto said.

'Major Wayne. Your witness.'

A bald major bore down briskly, all eyebrows and nostrils. A fraternal smile for Catto, who nodded and crossed his hands on his lap. 'You have some experience in the line, Lieutenant?'

'Yes sir. I came in in sixty-two and have been in the line since. Wounded at Stones River. Commissioned in the field.' Good of you to ask. My scars. Here and here.

'And therefore some discerning judgement, of your own men and the enemy as well.'

'Well, I wouldn't – '

'Now, now. This is not the time for modesty, Lieutenant.'

'All right. Yes.'

'You used the word "parole". Did you mean by that that the prisoner received the same treatment usually accorded rebel soldiers?'

'No sir. When any body of rebel soldiers was taken, we kept a close watch on them.'

'Ah. But a single prisoner? Say, one who had come over, as with your Dutchman.'

'Well, he'd be watched for a time, but then he'd be like one of us. Until we got back to a garrison.'

'So you treated the boy like one of those prisoners.'

'Yes sir.'

'Why was that?'

'What? Why was that?' After a moment of perplexity Catto said patiently, 'Well, he was a captured rebel soldier.'

'He had shot you. Did you treat him roughly?'

'No sir. Of course not.'

'Did you have reason to doubt his story?'

'You mean about Colonel Jessee?'

'Yes.'

'No. I've seen younger than that fighting. In regular Johnny regiments. Saw a boy about fourteen once with no legs.'

'Did you ever hear Cook's Guerrillas mentioned with reference to the boy?'

'No sir.'

'Where is Colonel Jessee now?'

'I have no idea, sir.'

In time, and with generous co-operation from his witness, the major made it plain that in better days Thomas Martin, like any handsome young soldier, would have been resplendent in grey, cap-a-pie, dashing, cool, one against hordes. After that first glance Catto had refrained from looking at the boy but did so in the end, and saw him wide-eyed, dazzled by visions of his own splendour. This accomplished, Catto was dismissed, stood to attention, faced about smartly, and strode to the door. There he turned in brief mutiny, said, 'Oh send him on home,' and skipped away like a brassy schoolboy.

A couple of nights later Catto entered the barracks almost unnoticed, ducking quickly out of a cold black silence into a yellow, fleshy, murmurous warmth; men sat, sprawled, lay; wrote, sang, read, played, dozed. Lowndes made love to his banjo. Catto's eyes went immediately to Haller, who sat smoking a pipe, and then to Godwinson, who frowned and scribbled. One of the two tables, sadly lame, seemed to be for scholars, the other for gamesters: he saw a checker-board. He was noticed then, and sound died slowly. Faces bloomed. The men were immobile; he felt their faintly malign hesitation. At length Haller rose and called the others to attention. Catto waited, bearing what he hoped was an expression of tolerant and amused despair. When they were all afoot he said, 'As you were,' and admired the general collapse.

'I have the feeling,' he said, 'that you better be a bit quicker and snappier now. I'm talking to the first platoon but you others may as well listen: I imagine I speak for Lieutenant Silliman too. Let's just see how fast you can get up, and how straight you can stand. Not that the army likes to impose on you. We appreciate your generosity in joining us here, and the sacrifice of your valuable time, and putting up with the food and all. But just the same. Now, then: attention!'

They leapt.

'Oh, much better,' he said, 'although the book seems out of place. What are you reading, Padgett?'

Padgett crimsoned; men snickered.

'Laughing, gentlemen? Laughing?' He had heard a major speak so once. 'What is it, Padgett?'

'It's *Come to Jesus*,' Padgett managed.

'Ah. By Doctor Newman Hall. The Christian Commission has been making its rounds. Well, we can't argue with that. But if anybody more important than a lieutenant walks in, you better just drop Jesus.'

'Yes sir.'

Catto, who was beginning to think himself a colonel, assumed an amiable solemnity. 'I want to say a few words. Settle down and keep quiet.' He waited. Groans. Clatter. They lit pipes and fanned smoke. How long, Catto wondered, since I have been alone? Have I ever in my life been alone?

'This will be a hard winter,' he began, 'and I am now going to tell you how to stay healthy and keep out of leg irons. You all know what the trouble is: the war is almost over and there isn't much for us to do. You're slobs to start with, and it will be worse now. First: report the least sign of sickness. Anything. Headache, a rash, whatever. The surgeon may send you right back, but there's plenty of quinine and no need to take chances. Then: bathe. Wash your filthy bodies. Keep your feet clean.' His gaze flickered to Franklin. 'And don't tell me you've heard all this before. You're the dirtiest bunch I've ever served with. There's barbers around. Use them. Keep the greybacks down. You'll be going to town now and then, and no sense straggling in like tramps. Also the surgeon tells me that the typhoid rate goes up every year, and not down.'

They shifted, scratched and primped.

'Now about keeping busy. When you're off duty, which will be most of the time, you can use books and games. You can write letters. You can keep your equipment in good order. You can even volunteer for odd jobs.' He received the gentle hoots with merry self-mockery, and cut them off with a wave. 'I was going to suggest that you study tactics – that's how Godwinson got his stripes – but it doesn't make too much sense now; this is probably the last war this country will ever fight. If you can find ways to catch up on your, ah, citizen occupations, go to it. Packages from home ought to be delivered on time now, and your letters will go out every day. Padgett's Christian Commission dumped a lot of paper and envelopes with the colonel; just ask. The colonel also has the names of some photographers in Cincinnati, if you want your picture in uniform. The price is listed and if they cheat you tell the colonel.

'Now.' He paused. 'Discipline.' For the moment they matched his gravity. 'You will have damn little to do for the next few months. Guard duty, mostly. The weekly inspection and the daily roll call. I want this barracks clean. Very clean. Not just no bugs, but soap clean. Other than that, you'll have days to fill. Weeks. Winter weeks too, with no chance to kick a ball around.

'That's the first thing. The second thing is General Hooker. He may never know you're here. He's a busy man. If he does hear about us, I'd like it to be for some, ah, complimentary reason. Not because Routledge has set fire to Cincinnati or Franklin has asphyxiated a roomful of people or one of you sharpers has cleaned out the Hundred Ninety-second at cards. Hooker is also a hard man, and unpredictable. So no horseplay with the corporal of the guard. Turn out on time and never mind the practical jokes. And no sitting down on guard, and don't leave your beat without relief. No noise after taps, and if you need a fight save it for a day in town. Let's have nobody hung up by his thumbs, or buck-and-gagged. You've got to be more careful because I'm an easy officer, so you can start practising on me: no more disrespect, and let's all call me sir at all times. I'll let you in on something: I want to stay in the army, it's the best home I ever had, and I don't want to be cut down to corporal when the war is over. That's partly up to you. So anybody who ever ate part of a pig I stole, or showed his ass and had nothing said about it – now's the time to pay me back. One more thing: don't ever sass an officer. Anything that sounds like a threat can win you a year in irons. If you brangle with an officer there's nothing I can do to help you. I'll toss you to the dogs. That goes for raiding the sutlers too.'

It was well done, he knew. A shame Phelan had not been present. Now the men were silent, concerned, almost frightened. With an evil smile Catto broke the mood: 'Hooker has nothing against whisky. I imagine there will be occasional distributions during the inclement season.'

This was followed by romp and hurrah, on which General Catto took his triumphant leave.

Next morning Colonel Bardsley told him that Thomas Martin had been found guilty of guerrilla activity and sentenced to be shot to death with musketry.

Chapter Three

Catto had not consorted much with generals, only that one impassioned chat with Rosecrans; about General August Willich he was uncertain. Deference might be proper; Willich was military commandant of Cincinnati. Easy fellowship might be proper: Willich had served with distinction at Shiloh and Stones River and Chickamauga and Chattanooga. Also Catto was curious about the useless arm. And then the general was a foreigner, a revolutionary in Germany about fifteen years before. Catto was of two minds about revolutionaries. Washington and Jefferson and Ethan Allen. All those names. John Hancock. But now times had changed, and those men were lauded, by stout officials on special occasions, in much the way that police chiefs and mayors were lauded. So he wondered about Willich.

Catto took a hitch in his trousers, once more admonished his inner devils, and advanced warily; he was properly amazed when Willich glowed and twinkled like every man's grandfather and spoke warmly: 'Catto. Good to see you, son. We should have met before; I hear you were wounded at Stones River. That was quite a time. Come and sit down.' They shook hands, Willich extending his left without awkwardness; the right arm hung limp, paralysed. Resaca, August, 1864; so short a time ago, this man was whole! Catto liked him immediately, instinctively, as one always tended to like another who reflected some feature, some quality, a strong nose or full lips or humour in the eyes. The general stood about six feet and was blond and blue-eyed and fair-skinned and bore an open and generous expression, sad, affectionate, the wrinkles of a man, the eyes and mouth of a boy. 'Been wounded again since, hey? Tell me what I can do for you.'

Catto mumbled. This heartiness was irregular. Approaching

Willich had been in the nature of a hard climb, a short but slippery step to the shoulder of one suspicious captain, a leap then to a bored and indifferent lieutenant-colonel, a slip side-wise to the adjutant, a day's wait for regrouping and provisioning, and here he was with this warm and friendly gentleman, slightly rumpled, who called him son. Catto seated himself. The room was more like a parlour or a banker's office than a general's headquarters: a desk, a sofa, several armchairs, a few engravings of horses and game-birds, a cabinet. No crossed sabres, no racked rifles. Willich himself seemed about to potter, to pull out a feather duster and set to work. He rubbed his hands and smiled. 'A cigar?'

'Why, thank you. Sir.'

'You've earned a cigar. I don't use them myself.' Willich tossed him a thick phosphorous match; Catto struck it on a button (Damn! Wrong thing to do!) and waited for the gases to dissipate. 'I see you turned down a colonelcy with the Twenty-fifth Corps.'

Catto blew smoke, and examined the lighted cigar in manly fashion. 'Yes sir. It was quite a temptation. But I don't much like them. Sort of uneasy around them. Never saw one till I was about twelve. And they're temporary, I imagine; why else would anyone offer a colonelcy to a young fellow like me? And where would I be later when they took my black heroes away from me and sent them home?'

'Yes. I understand. However. You have business.'

'Yes.' Catto was relieved and emboldened. 'The boy Thomas Martin has been sentenced to death. You know about that?'

Willich nodded and looked owlish.

'That's a terrible thing for grown men to do.' Catto went on.

'Oh it is, it is,' Willich told him gravely.

Catto scowled. 'Well then, well then – ' He bit down on the cigar.

'You take that seriously,' the general said.

'I do,' said Catto. 'I am the one he shot and I am the one who brought him in. He is a poor country boy who cannot read or write, and is the next thing to an orphan, and wouldn't know

Mister Lincoln from Jeff Davis. If you don't mind my saying so, General, I am damned upset about this.'

'Well, I think I do mind,' said Willich. 'In the first place, bad language never saved a lost cause.'

'I apologize,' Catto said stiffly.

'And in the second place, the boy has already been paroled in my charge.' Willich was grinning. Catto cursed himself for a fool. Willich said, 'He has already polished my boots half a dozen times, and carried a message to Judge Stallo – halfway across Cincinnati without a guard! – and returned promptly with an answer. He is saving his tips and will surely be a success in later life.'

'I'm a fool,' Catto said.

'Ah. Then go back one step and try to think like a general. Do you know that there are still a thousand guerrillas in Kentucky? Even in southern Illinois? Illinois was settled mainly by southerners. Those people can do great damage. The death sentence has become automatic, but only to deter, only as a caution. It would hardly do to let them feel that they could kill and burn with impunity.'

'But the boy wasn't a guerrilla.'

'We cannot be sure. We resolved the doubt in our own favour; in favour of innocent people who are potential victims. That we must do. We had no choice.'

'But the boy.' Catto's confusion deepened.

'I interviewed the boy when they brought him in,' Willich said. 'For heaven's sake, Catto, what must you think of me? The court-martial was necessary. The verdict was necessary. The boy will have the freedom of the city and will do odd jobs for my staff. When the war ends I will give him a gold piece and a suit of clothes and send him home.'

'For God's sake,' Catto sighed.

'You astound me, Lieutenant. A man of your talents. Now look here. In Germany I was almost killed – I was exiled, did you know that? – fighting for a republic, and against the censorship, and for life's good things for all. And here I was an editor, a good newspaper, the *Deutsche Republikaner* right here in the city, and I tell you, what I care most about is injustice. All my life. Why am I here? With this useless wing?' Willich had grown vehement; Catto nodded respectfully. 'Well, well,' said the general. 'So. You see. Why would you want to stay in the army if the army was what you seem to think it is?'

'Now how did you know that? Sir.'

'Generals hear things. The army is people, and people are not bad, my boy. Do you think a man like Abraham Lincoln would sign an order for that boy's execution? Ah, no. Ah, no.'

Again Catto nodded. 'That occurred to me. But he's a long way off. Maybe,' and he grinned ingratiatingly at his own impudence, 'it's because I'm a good lieutenant: an order is an order. So I didn't believe – '

'But you are not a good lieutenant,' Willich said primly. 'You are known, to me and others, as an easy officer and somewhat puppyish.'

Aghast, Catto sat silent.

'On the other hand, your men have fought well and none have deserted. So maybe you are not such a bad lieutenant after all, hey? You see, generals are not fools. In that, times have changed. When I was your age all generals were fools.'

Catto nodded sheepishly.

'Was there anything else?' Willich was now merely polite.

'Yes.' Catto cleared his throat. 'Yes sir, there is. I have a Jonah named Routledge, over forty, has nine children at home. He's more trouble than he's worth and I want to see if I can get him out of the army.'

Willich's brows rose, came to half-mast, rose again.

'It just makes no sense having him here,' Catto said.

'Well, that's another problem.' Willich's tone was encouraging, intimate; Catto experienced a tickle of hope. 'What makes sense, and what does not.' Hope died. 'It depends on who is deciding, does it not. However. Over forty, you say. Large family. I'll look into it. Anything else?'

'No sir. Happy to have met you at last and I hope I've been no bother.' Catto had wanted a warmer note but his tongue, or his heart, failed him.

'My pleasure, Lieutenant. Good day to you.'

Catto went out cursing himself, not sure why, needing hulla-

46

balloo and uproar to drown out a sharp and nagging inner voice, the voice of failure, of pomposity; the cracking voice of a pimpled schoolboy. Within him, mysterious calefactions, moral cramps. He stomped across a parade ground, lowering and dour, and sure enough, the thought came, adding shame to his other perplexities, quandaries and conundrums: *God damn them all!* He looked about him, an action unwilled and irresistible, but he was alone.

Still, he had accomplished a morning's work. Converse with a general; the boy safe; a word in for Routledge. Not to mention a fine cigar; he drew on it briskly now, and frowned slightly to give himself importance. He felt rather a new man, one whose circle of acquaintances included those of the highest rank and attainment; one who had single-handed saved Thomas Martin; one who was shipping Routledge home, with a hearty grip of the hand and a few sound aphorisms. His stomp altered to a swagger. Vanity, vanity.

'I suppose I must accustom myself to this doing nothing.' He launched a greasy ring of cigar smoke, domestic this time, hours later; it undulated briefly in the yellow light, floated to Phelan's cluttered table, ringed a phial, writhed, clung, decomposed, vanished.

'Not bad,' Phelan said. 'I wish the flesh would behave so. Leave not a rack behind. Your boys were burying horses today. Some of them anyway. The big fellow with a beard.'

'Routledge. Probably buried his own foot by mistake, and is still out there wondering what to do about it. Is there a medical term for people who never do anything right?'

'Doctors,' Phelan said. 'Here is a young lady who describes herself as twenty, minister's daughter, cultured, seeking to cheer a military gentleman with news from home.'

'A spinster. Doomed to the single life. Bad complexion,' and Catto went on quickly, avoiding Phelan's eye, 'bow legs, doubtless overweight. What newspaper is that?'

'The *Gazette*. You make her sound like those female nurses. Did I tell you of the official requirements?'

'No. Nothing under sixty, I suppose.'

'Wait,' Phelan scrabbled among documents. 'Here we are. Listen now, because this shows that Washington is on to you. "Past thirty",' he read. ' "healthy, plain almost to repulsion in dress, and devoid of personal attractions".'

'That would be going some,' Catto growled. 'In my present state Surgeon Phelan is not devoid of personal attractions.'

'Dear me. But we are of different faiths.'

Catto sat up, swung his unshod feet to the floor, hunched forward. 'Jack. I want to ask you something. Tell me about the smallpox.'

'The smallpox?' Phelan tossed aside his newspaper. 'At this time of night? Well, it is still a problem. All the conditions – '

'No. Yours.'

'Mine?' Phelan blinked and mulled. 'Ah no. I see what you're at. This is not smallpox.'

'Oh. I'm sorry. I thought – '

'Of course you did. I don't mind. No, no. This is merely the chicken pox, my friend. As experienced by a young man of four, in a family of eight living in one room, in a house of twelve rooms, in each a family of six or so. A house surrounded by many other such houses, served by pumps in the street and earth closets. I was lucky it was not the black plague. That is what they call the ould sod. Although the country folk had it better.'

'God. You were lucky to get out.'

'I got out at eighteen, when it was too late. My brothers and sisters never got out, though four of them were lucky enough to die young. There were three more, you know, who died the first month. Hearth and home. The Anglo-Irish provided charity each Christmas, in joyous celebration of the birth of our Lord.'

'I know. I had nine years in a home for orphans.'

'Nasty little buggers, no doubt.'

'Yessir. And perishing cold, believe me. We used to fight just to keep warm.' He laughed awkwardly and blushed.

'Oho. What have you remembered?'

Catto laughed frankly then, in hoots and roars. 'Buggers is right. The vilest set of moral cripples in the United States of America.'

Phelan applauded. 'Now that's a lovely phrase, from you.'

Catto was still red. 'There was a lady used to come with exhortations three or four times a week. God and the good life and so forth. She used to hug us. She hugged all of us, so nobody was any worse embarrassed than anybody else. She was a good stout lady with a great soft bosom, and she had the trick of pulling your head right in there in between. Some of us used to line up twice. Those over twelve.'

Phelan was cackling.

'And the food. I eat better in the army. Sometimes I'm sick to my stomach just remembering that food.'

'Ah. Unlike me you never knew the ecstasies of family life.' Phelan pulled a sour face. 'I wish to God my own mother had been blessed with a bosom. She was a broomstick and spent her life half-starved. I pass over any mention of the food itself. The garbage in New York was tastier. New York was paradise.'

'How'd you get there?'

'Jumped ship. Which is why I signed on. I was, if you can believe it, rather a bright boy, and won a certificate from the fathers, which impressed the captain of some tub out of Cork. Oh, I was sick.'

'Well, I'm glad you made it.'

'And now I am an honoured member of a respected profession. I never sent a penny home and never wrote. Damn them all.'

'You don't mean that.'

'I mean it, all right. I never asked to be born, and starved, and disfigured. I can't even grow a decent beard to hide the damn things. I tried once and it looked like the mange. The ladies are very polite.'

Catto brooded. 'The ladies. God damn it, Jack. They drive me crazy.'

'Yes. We are born with these great cannon and no work for them. Did you ever have a look at a new-born baby boy? Enormous equipment. There is something mysterious about it: animals have their heats and such, and go sniffing about in their seasons, but men must be trained to decent behaviour. We are always ready. Give us five minutes with nothing to do and we start moaning and scratching ourselves. Or burying ourselves in fat bosoms at the age of twelve. Well, boy, that's the way of it. And it's worse here. An army of scruffy, ill-bred louts with time on their hands. They'll have something else on their hands every night.'

'Not me,' Catto said stiffly. 'I'm too old for that.'

'Oh no. Too scared. Hell-fire or whatever. But you're right. Save it for the ladies. You'll enjoy it all the more. Now I wish you would let me get on with my studies here. I am looking for an advertisement by a beautiful young woman with a figger like Juno and ungovernable passions, in desperate need of an expert, pockmarked Irish surgeon of thirty-four. Her father must be a rich distiller with old-fashioned beliefs like the dowry.'

'Ask her if she has a sister,' Catto said. He groaned feebly. 'Or even a widowed grandmother.'

Catto was a virgin. Virgins existed in those days. One of his great fears had been that he would die a virgin. The fear sprang not from any desire to leave descendants, but from lecherous curiosity and a poor orphan's sense of waste. The death of a virgin was to Catto inexpressibly sad, being also a contradiction, a contravention of natural law, an unfulfilment, a betrayal of logic, of nature itself, something in it of the house that burns the day they finish glazing, or the pumpkin pie fumbled, hot from the oven, spang on the day's heap of dust, scraps and mouse droppings. And it was easy enough to die a virgin. Millions of young people were carried off betimes by a merciful Providence, catapulted directly to the Good Place and spared poxes, thumbscrews, suppurations – and raptures. In war, yes, many. And woman was, as much as death, an ultimate mystery; sad to miss the one when the other was inevitable. Catto, in whom motive and means flourished, had lacked opportunity and courage. First because in an orphanage administered by God, or by his canting surrogates, young gentlemen tended to find pleasure in one another; Catto was fifteen before he spoke a single serious word to a female under thirty-five, and his seduction was accomplished not by a buxom, raven-haired beauty out of Walter Scott, much less by some fair, inaccessible Rowena, but by a plumpish rogue called Chester. And then because he was afraid, intensely afraid, not precisely of God (Catto was uncertain about God, and at best vexed with Him), but of lightnings, thunders, witherings, castrations and simple horse-whippings. Also of failure, and of unspecified marks of shame: a scarlet letter, boils, a permanent erection necessitating bespoke britches. And then came the war, and camp-followers, with many men behaving like animals, and Catto saw no reason not to join them, really, having long thought of himself as a mutt, a hybrid of the better beasts, lone wolf, gay dog, young cock, Tom Catto; but he made a discovery, a most inopportune, piteous and calamitous discovery: he was a coward. His coward-ice took the form of a haughty belief in his own singularity, which kept him off public conveyances, so to speak, and left him waiting endlessly on crowded corners for cabs that never came. The dreams and fantasies that now and again overmastered him were trite; the evasions and lies that permitted him to live on terms of manly equality with the Phelans of the world – those painful twists and strains so alien to a young, direct, apparently uncomplicated man – left his withers always badly wrung; they were voluntary and public, and therefore more shameful than his incorrigible private passions. But he knew no 'nice' girls, who were anyway not to be so rudely thought of; and in 1863 a special hospital had been established in Louisville for the treatment of venereal tragedies: the tales were harrowing. Rumour, gossip, myth, loneliness: these were what he (and more others than would confess) knew of fleshly love. Or for that matter of ethereal love. Marriage would, someday, be natural and necessary and doubtless even pleasant, and marriage implied – though Catto was of two minds about this – a creature soft, ignorant, fragile and vulnerable, above all vulnerable, whose bruising destiny it was to submit to pain and indignity, and whom it was simply not fair to sully with the residue, the leavings, of past concupiscence. (The very word, concupiscence, in use among the clergy, appalled him.) Catto had sufficient sin in his heart – those throbs of pleasure at a good shot that took a life – and felt that other slates might better be kept clean. He was always kind to children, as became a hero.

So this lieutenant fought his own war too, moving through

company streets on nippy fall evenings, the sun just down, the cold air with its hint of smoke quickening his breath and blood so that his body blazed and then ached, desiring unknown warmths, as though he bore, slung in his trousers, a cold, hungry bear cub, so cold, so hungry, that often Catto turned away from his companions, from himself, with moist eyes as a deep, murderous, clutching emptiness annihilated him. 'Just thinking about a girl I knew,' he would say, and Phelan would chuckle and tell him, 'Ah, my boy, if I had your youth and vigour,' and they would go on to talk of other things.

Yet it was not all bad. Catto had sense enough to recognize the glory of expectations, and to suspect fulfilments, and sense enough to know that if sufficient generations honoured any state of mind or body (God looks after naturals) there might indeed be something honourable in it. I wish I had a girl, he would think; someone to save it *for;* virtue in a vacuum was not easy. Virtue, virtue, virtue my ass, he would think, and add round expletives, as men do when profoundly embarrassed, making inner noises, profane and loud, to distract themselves, to drive off a shameful memory or an unwelcome truth. And he breathed the chill night, calming himself, remembering that he was a lieutenant of infantry and so forth. Give me time, he decided, and I will do a bit better. At the notion of a future he wondered again what that wife of his might be like. Honey-coloured hair, he hoped, colour of eyes unimportant, but a fine figger, she must be a fine figger; and that brought him to the beginning again, to his avid, detached, hovering lusts, and he saw himself trapped in a circle of want and wait, wax and wane, will and wont. So marched heavily back to his cabin, his men, a nip of whisky, a game of cards. The cards eased him, fifty-two of them flying about the blanket like birds in patterns, five fluttering into his hand, raising and relieving small excitements, and the money, bits and pieces and scraps of scrip to bet, to win, to count, to stack and stow, and if all the woman he had tonight was the smallest corner of a pasteboard queen, squeezing slowly into sight after the draw, he unsure if she was one of his original pair and then knowing she was a red-headed stranger, glancing in spite of himself at the glittering

52

money in the yellow lamplight – well, if that was all he had tonight it was better than a ball in the belly, and it was no small consolation to know that he had survived. Where there's life there's hope, he thought, as Silliman laid down three aces.

'Well this is a galled jade they have given me,' Phelan said.

'It's a dark night,' Catto said. 'You don't want a horse too frisky on a night like this, and a little snow in the air too.' He trembled with excitement, and thanked God that Phelan could not see it.

'Nobody else out, anyway.'

They trotted along, just north of the city, no starlight and no moonlight but a faint glow all about them. Now and then a spark of lamplight, a farmhouse. Catto shifted in the saddle, perturbed. Fires on the hearth. Father and Mother and Little Willie and Baby Mary. 'God damn,' he said aloud. 'God damn,' but the vision persisted. 'What's wrong?' Phelan asked. 'Nothing,' Catto said. He saw the kitchen, a long, solid wooden table, a tremendous fire in a tremendous stone fireplace. Around the table ruddy faces, in the warm air warm smells: burning wood, charred meat, leek soup. Catto blinked, and contracted in mysterious embarrassments. A cold night, November, winter closing in.

Well, all right, it would be not bad. Leek soup. Hot potatoes and butter. Worth saying grace.

He considered some future Catto, father of seven. You, Little Willie, chew with your mouth shut. Baby Mary, come here for a pat.

His face was warm in the freezing air. Where did a man pat his own daughter? Fool. This is your home. This blue suit. That's all. Even the horse is only borrowed.

'Not long now,' Phelan sang out. They clattered across a bridge. 'Check small arms.'

It was true: in the distance Catto saw a light. A mile, two. He drew in a deep breath, and the cold air seared, and abruptly his body was hot, and there was a deep, flickering, lapping ache in his belly, and all upon him, as if he lay at the bottom of the sea, yearning for air, dizzy and dying. He blinked again, firmly, and brought his knees tighter against the horse. He wondered again what she would look like. Smell like. Better than leek soup? Cold air streamed beneath his collar; he hunched; Phelan had led him into a canter and he had not really noticed. Quick! Quick!

And there they were, whickering into the stable-yard like a couple of knights-errant, with a hostler emerging to take the reins, and Phelan dismounting with all the grace and non-chalance of some silly dook somewhere, as if he would fling the man a bag of silver. Faint odours steamed from the inn, contended briefly with manure, lost, regrouped, steamed forth again. Catto had never seen, or smelled, or heard so clearly; his fingertips tingled. 'Pound for pound,' he said, 'I am the strongest man in the whole world.'

'That's right.' Phelan said. 'Just behave now.' An oil-lamp glowed above the door, another on the porch. Phelan strode in; Catto shut the door carefully, and removed his hat timidly. They stood in a bright hallway, before them a grand staircase rising wide, curving both ways like a ram's horns; to the right and left of them were doors, a saloon, a dining-room. Upon a polished table, candlesticks, a dancing flower of light. 'Some house, hey? It was once a rich man's.'

'I believe that.'

From the saloon peered a slight man of some distinction; his hair was brushed, his shirt ruffled. He was bare of whiskers, and wore black. 'Jack Phelan.'

'Hello, host. This is Lieutenant Catto.'

'How do,' Catto said.

Their host bowed. 'Stanley. Give me your hats and coats. Gloves. There's a bottle of the best inside. Go on. Ladies be along shortly.'

The saloon was properly dark, three or four candelabra, and a low fire in a long stone fireplace. Catto, jittery, stepped to the fireplace and performed traditional rubs, claps and hand-wringings until he realized that he was not at all cold. 'God's sake,' he said, 'give me a drink.'

The barkeep, who might have been Stanley's brother, announced that his name was Horgan and handed a bottle to

Phelan. 'All alone tonight,' Phelan said.

'Place is yours,' Horgan agreed.

With bottle and glasses and boots Phelan clinked and creaked to a table: he drew the cork, whisky flowed. 'Drink, boy. This is more like.'

But Catto paused. He sniffed the whisky, and dipped the tip of his tongue, and then stood calming his flutter, telling himself that he was a silly fellow: this was a beautiful night in November, a fitting fall night, and there was not a man in the house that he could not put down if necessary, and there were steaks and ladies to look forward to. So there was no need for shakes, and no need to force himself into the evening with quick whisky, and really no need to think of this, or of himself, as unusual. A soldier's night. No: an officer's night. And by God! but I am glad to be an officer! Eat, drink, be merry, for tomorrow you will not die, and what is the sense of living if you cannot eat, drink and be merry?

Phelan raised his glass. 'Now what are you thinking of?'

'Whisky and women,' Catto said lazily. 'I was wondering if you wanted advice.'

Phelan jeered silently and said, 'I know your kind. Ignorant and blustery.'

'I can't be ignorant. I spent ten years in school and was given a certificate.'

'And what did you learn?' Phelan sipped whisky; his eyes roved. He was not listening much.

But then Catto, also sipping whisky, was not talking to be heard. 'I can read and write, and spell pretty well, and multiply and divide. I know where babies come from and I know where the continents are. I know some Latin words like *amicus amici* and *omnis morris*. The orphanage taught me all that, also to be on time for meals.'

'Even Australia?'

'Especially Australia.'

'That's not bad. You see there is something to be said for institutions.'

'Yeh.' Catto drank again and was suddenly, almost miraculously, calm. Slightly amused. After all. Just whores. And that

Stanley is only a pimp and this mansion is only a fancy house.

The whisky stung merrily inside him, and life took on a certain clarity. There were eighteen several candles in this room. He had been shot twice and had killed eleven times for sure. He had no living kin that he knew of. He was handsome, with light brown hair, now and again reddish, and brown eyes and a ruddy face and a bushy moustache and a handsome, almost hooked, highland nose. Not merely handsome but handsome in a notably healthy way; not like a pale handsome Frenchman. But there must be red-faced Frenchmen too. 'Horgan. Bring us some apples.'

'Good God.'

'I like apples. Leave me be.'

He was mercurial and sanguinary, as the almanacs had it, of noble port, and demeaned himself well in society. At the moment he was in the pink in all respects, and had washed with soap. With the war over, for most purposes, and apples arriving for his private tooth. He began – it lasted only a moment – to grope towards honest thought; always this man was within me, and what I was was the beginning of what I am, and someone else is still in the making here, with the rules and patterns already laid out.

It was almost inevitable that he would someday be a general, and wear a purfled hat. 'Some day,' he said, and stopped. Horgan had come to set a dish of apples upon the grainy table.

'Some day what?'

'Nothing. You're quiet tonight.'

'I am not here to entertain lieutenants,' Phelan said. 'I was thinking of maggots and my own wisdom.'

'Ah. Surgeons know everything.'

'Surgeons know nothing,' Phelan began. He saw Catto's eyes then, and turned.

The door had opened and two ladies were entering. Good God, Catto thought, as he was burned alive. These are *beautiful.* These are not just whores. These are *lady* whores.

He proved to be perfectly right. The one with black hair glared. 'Hodja do,' she enunciated. 'Do you not rise?'

Some hours later Catto whispered, 'Listen,' low and urgent, 'help me. Please. Teach me things.'

'Oh you great bull,' she breathed in retail delight, 'oh you hot lover,' and he grinned in the dark and judged himself a devilish sly fellow, though uncomfortably breathless and scared silly of sin.

Chapter Four

Often that winter they saw Thomas Martin on a mule, the brainless beast ('But horses are dumber,' the boy said) shuffling through the snow at dusk, slipping here and there on the hard-packed company streets. The boy was usually in a wool cap, a heavy sweater under the blue blouse, knit gloves, winter blue trousers, stout halfboots. He knew his way about, even outside the city, and delivered promptly: messages, small parcels, incidental greetings, once a sack of mail ('That's illegal,' he said, almost proudly). And confidential intelligence: turning a corner one December day, his mule almost ran Catto down, but the boy hauled up with a grin and chirruped, 'Hey, Lieutenant! How's your shoulder?'

'Good as new,' Catto assured him. 'How's yourself?'

'Very good. Got a steady job with the general. I eat right and I sleep warm.' The boy giggled. 'Those loads of knit goods come in from old ladies and churches, and he sees to it I get first pick. This sweater.' He unbuttoned the blouse and Catto admired a heavy yellow cable-stitched pullover with a collar that unrolled to become a hood. 'Fine and dandy, hey?'

'Pretty good,' Catto said. 'Smartest thing you ever did was get yourself caught. Probably eat better than you did at home.'

'That's a fact.' The boy smiled, and Catto saw again that innocence, that careless and uncomplicated acceptance of pain or joy. 'More snow coming. Where's Jacob?'

'No idea. Haven't seen him for days.'

'I'll find him. Tell you what, Lieutenant.'

'Tell me.'

'The Fifth Indiana got a thousand bushels of apples. All piled up in the cold.'

'That right.'

'That's right.'

They kept silence for a bit, Catto nodding and considering, the boy hunched forward almost between the mule's ears, staring innocently at Catto with the dead pan of the true conspirator. 'That's interesting,' Catto said. 'You don't happen to smoke cigars?'

'Nope. But I know someone who does.'

'Have one. Take care of yourself, boy.'

'Good-bye, Lieutenant.'

So with Haller and four men and a wagon, all very military, orders ringing out, colonels' names invoked, 'Work fast, move in, load up, move out, nobody talks but me,' Catto made away with fifty bushels of Albemarle pippins, forty-eight of which reached his men. 'Very good,' Phelan said. 'Anti-scorbutic, for one thing, and it beats spuds, onions and dried turnips.'

'What's a spud?'

'A potato. You never heard that?'

'Never.'

They were munching Catto's private stock in Phelan's tepee, by the light of a couple of candles. Phelan's blouse was off; he was lolling in a red wool shirt, unmilitary and unmedical. 'How's the shoulder?'

'Why? You got some hungry worms?'

Phelan cackled. 'Still offended, are you?'

'It made me feel like meat.'

'You are meat. Only the divine soul makes you different from a hog.'

'That again.'

Phelan's glance exiled him: it was the glance of a man who looked not at but beyond, and it expressed indifference, superiority, certainty, pity – all those at once. It was dissolved by a smile. 'Yes. That again. Someday you'll know. In fifty years the whole world will be Catholic again.'

'Ah yes.' Catto parried: 'Have you heard the latest about the Ninetieth Illinois?'

Phelan puckered in grief.

'A certain Sergeant Houlihan,' Catto went on, 'drilling his men, and at the end of his rope, he was, they were that awkward, and he says to them, he says. "Phwat a ragged line, bhoys! Come over here and take a look at yerselves!" '

Phelan bellowed and jubilated, 'I hate you for it,' he said at last, 'but it's a good one. And you do it well enough, you do. Somewhere back there was a Bridget or a Paddy.' He cackled a bit more.

'Och aye,' said Catto drily.

'Okay indeed,' Phelan said.

Catto met Hooker after all, on an afternoon in January. The seeker after wisdom was lallygagging about with Silliman, losing thousands at head-to-head stud, 'You cheat. You must cheat.'

'Never.' Silliman popped a pastille past his avaricious grin, and sucked. 'Just natural born lucky.'

'What are those candies?'

'Cherry drops. M'mother sends them. Take some. One hundred dollars on the ace-king.'

Catto pondered invective; at a thunderous tattoo both officers started like rabbits. 'Come in,' Catto bawled.

It was Godwinson. 'Lieutenant.'

'Yeh. Hello. What?'

'At the barracks. General Hooker.'

Catto's first thought was, Thank God I shaved. 'Here? Out here in the country?' He was already up and bustling, and so was Silliman: buttons, greatcoat, hat, cockade bobbing. They hit the company street with a stamp and a clatter; they might have struck sparks from the frozen earth. Halfway to the barracks Catto remembered to thank Godwinson. 'When did he come?'

'Just a few minutes ago. I slipped out right away.'

'Yeh. You studied tactics.'

From Silliman a bubble of mockery.

'You laugh,' Catto puffed. 'But you piled out fast enough. And you've got that yessir-nossir look on your face. Ramrod up the ass.'

'I favour a more refined manner of speech,' Silliman said.

'God Almighty. These are critical times.'

'What do we do?'

'Bounce right in,' Catto said after a moment. 'We don't know he's there.'

'Fine. You first.'

'Damn right. No. Godwinson, go in first and get them up.'

'They'll be up.'

'I know that. But make the right noises. Here we are – in you go.'

And in he went, Godwinson; flung the door wide and bellowed 'Ten-shah!' and the lieutenants came striding in like a colour picture from a boy's book, *Our Union Heroes*, one ruddy and moustached and big, the young bull, the other blond with no hair on his face, slim, elegant, handsome, almost dapper and delicate, the golden colt. Their men were frozen in pairs before the double-decked bunks, and far down the aisle, near the stove, there flourished a stand of officers. Catto and Silliman clacked to attention as one, saluted as one, and Catto saw the poster, Music Hall, *Tonight* Catto & Silliman *Simultaneous Acrobatics and Manoeuvres* A Colourful Display of Extraordinary Precision *Also Charlotte's Arabian Dance*, but pulled himself together in time. Hooker returned their salute.

Catto liked him cautiously. Hooker was a handsome man and had not run to fat. He was rosy-cheeked and not weather-beaten; he had dark hair, carelessly trimmed, curling out beneath his hat; and blue eyes. An aide murmured. 'Lieutenant Catto,' Hooker said amiably. The men were shockingly still, like wax exhibits; a chill plucked at Catto. 'Sir,' he said. 'And Lieutenant Silliman.' 'Sir.' Waxworks, the air of a morgue. One of Hooker's aides was young, a captain, tall and fair, smiling a thin, overly pleasant smile. The other two were majors.

'You've done well,' Hooker said. 'Nobody was drunk, these gloves are still white, I see no spit on the floor. Despite your distance from headquarters.' Catto glowed; a rainbow of decorations sprouted on his breast, stars, sunbursts, golden crosses. 'At ease, by the way.' The two relaxed stiffly. 'All of you.' Hooker said, not raising his voice, and the men slumped and settled as if they had been warmed. 'However,' Hooker said, 'there is one problem. Perhaps you'd like to come over here.'

The two marched forward, grave, all business, and then, only then, Catto saw Haller at the foot of his bunk, masked by the officers, now unmasked, his face empty of all expression save fury, and even the fury visible only to Catto. 'You know Sergeant Haller, of course,' Hooker said mildly. 'Well, here we were, conducting an informal inspection, keeping in touch with the troops.' He was beardless, affecting long sideburns; below the rosy cheeks his half day's growth of whisker was black. Some days he would shave twice. 'And Captain Dunglas here,' still smiling his thin, overly pleasant smile, at Captain Dunglas, who bowed slightly, 'thought to take a look inside that chest under the bunk. I don't suppose you could guess what he found.'

'No sir.'

Hooker stared for a moment at Haller, the damning neutral glance, the blue eyes cold. 'He found several pounds of coffee, and several pounds of sugar, and some tea; twenty-two small candles, seventeen bars of yellow soap, and four pairs of brand-new boots size nine.'

Catto's mind shuffled replies, all inadequate. After a time the swollen silence grew painful.

'Did you know of this?'

Catto waited too long, so long that he deprived himself of choice and found the truth necessary. 'Yes sir.'

'You almost lied.' Hooker was inspecting him, and soon Catto ceased to take refuge in eyes-front, and looked full at him.

'Yes sir. I almost lied.'

'Tell me about it.'

Catto fought to keep his head clear. Hooker ignored the others. He made Catto feel that this was something between the two of them, as if they had been through many campaigns together and these other soldiers were of no importance. He invited affection, confidence and confidences, truth, order, a kind of official serenity; you see, he seemed to be saying, we share powers and obligations.

'General, could we dismiss the men?'

'I think not,' Hooker said. 'Tell me why you told the truth.'

'All right,' Catto said. 'If I had said no, the responsibility would still have been mine. But you would have come down hard on him and I wouldn't have been able to speak up for him.'

'Ah. Then you told the truth not simply because it was the truth.' Still he ignored the others.

'No sir. I would have lied if it would have done him any good. But it wouldn't have helped.'

'I see,' Hooker nodded thoughtfully. 'Then if you knew about it, why didn't you stop it?'

'Because he's my best soldier,' Catto said, 'and he's been in the army a long time, and he's gone without coffee and tea and sugar and shoes longer than the rest of us all together – my platoon, I mean. He's the army. We can manage without lieutenants but not without sergeants. If he wants to be his own quartermaster it's because the army's taught him he has to. He can't trust his officers. It's not for me to turn him in. Sir.' Catto shut up then, too late, he knew.

Hooker nodded again, staring off into some other year; then he glanced sharply at Catto and turned to his aides. Dunglas was smiling away. 'Reduction to private,' Hooker said. 'Buck and gag for twelve hours, to start tomorrow at reveille. The stolen goods to be distributed among the men of this platoon before his eyes.'

'General!'

'Lieutenant Catto,' Hooker's voice fell among them like sleet.

Catto's anger kept pace with his fear; for one brief and awful instant his gaze and Hooker's blazed up, and Catto's died first. He turned away. 'Dammit, Haller, haven't you anything to say for yourself?'

They all watched the old sergeant, this small man, a bit wizened but with an air of survival about him. He stood, permanent, untouchable, faintly baleful, like a statue at the entrance to a military cemetery. When he spoke it was to Hooker. 'I was a private in Mexico when you were a lieutenant-colonel down there. I've been in the army every day of my life since I was eighteen. What the lieutenant says is right. I done without. I see these paper-collar soldiers with money from home – '

'That's enough,' Hooker said. 'Buck and gag for six hours, then.'

'His stripes, General,' Catto was firm.

'Reduction to private,' Hooker repeated, with a trace of impatience. 'And I want a word with you, Lieutenant. This way, please. Not you, Silliman.'

'Let us walk together a way,' the general said. 'You others follow along behind.'

Out of doors, Catto cooled; only pride kept him impassive. He quaked. Fool!

'Cold. I don't like the winter out here.'

Catto muttered.

'You're a goddam fool, Lieutenant.'

Catto found the courage to be silent.

'Discipline isn't only a matter of keeping order in battle. Or even of habit. We discipline some to protect the others. As simple as that. Why bother to follow orders, if others can contravene and go scot-free? When a sergeant steals, a private goes hungry. I will not have my men go hungry. I will not have my sentries sleeping. I will not have courtesy neglected, and I will not have rank ignored. You were close enough to insolence back there, as you are now, with that childishly surly expression, and by your refusal to face a superior officer when addressed.' Catto turned immediately, though there seemed little he could do about the surly expression; he moderated it to fretful. 'I spare you an official reprimand for one reason only: you stood up for your own sergeant. An officer who will not stand up for his own men – against the enemy, against a general,' and Hooker was frowning, flapping his gloved hands, glaring at Catto, 'against Lincoln himself – *Lincoln would not let me shoot a sleeping sentry*. Because the boy's mother wept. Bah! That sentry jeopardized a whole regiment.' Hooker bore himself now like a man in great physical pain; his step slowed. '*My men*, I was responsible for every man-jack of them – to the country, to their wives, to their children – and that sentry slept . . . Well.' Hooker stepped out again, and flashed a friendly smile at Catto. 'You see. I value an officer who will take care of his own. Pride. I cannot tell you too often how important is pride. You know I am responsible for the system of corps badges.' It was a wild, rakish air he had, marred, Catto noticed, by the beginnings of a double chin. A lady-killer for sure. Hooker sucked in a great swallow of cold air. 'By God. I need the healing draught. You're dismissed, Lieutenant Catto.'

Catto came to attention and saluted. Hooker saluted formally in return, and for a moment his eyes burned icily at Catto's: 'Buck and gag, Lieutenant. Six hours. See to it. Don't ever try to shit a general.'

'No sir,' Catto dropped his salute, faced about, and strode off, profoundly shocked.

The morrow did not dawn bright; as Phelan put it, Phoebus' fiery chariot never left the barn. The army was shouted awake by its corporals, who had been routed out by the guard when the hired cock declined to crow: at ten degrees below zero buglers balked. Without benefit of their morning call a shivering mob emerged, keening and complaining, leaning together, eyes half shut, uniforms half on half off, one boot on a foot, one in a hand, blouses and greatcoats unbuttoned. The usual calls of nature evoked the usual impatient groans and gavottes. Carlsbach was in full and proper uniform because he was a Minuteman: he slept dressed. 'Saves time on retreats.' Routledge shuffled out whimpering; genuine tears froze on his cheeks. Piggy Franklin, rheumy, was sustained by the hope of a whisky-and-quinine before breakfast. From a barracks doorway Catto observed, not without loathing, this malodorous rabble. He and Silliman and the boy Padgett were well turned out, because this week Padgett was their orderly and had risen an hour before the others to report at the officers' little cabin by half past five, bearing a kettle of hot water and a bucket of cold so that the officers could rise, dash to the officers' sink, dash back, and perform the necessary ablutions in relative comfort. Like most orderlies Padgett cheated his way into the officers' sink (who cared, at that hour?), which was indoors and boasted an iron stove, so that if he took the corner seat he could even warm his hands while pooing. He was famous for that, though his comrades were men enough to keep it within the company: 'I got to poo,' he said one day, and in utter silence every man laid down his tool, cigar, checker, ramrod, plug, pamphlet, pen: 'You got to what?' Padgett said it again. When Carslbach said later, 'Come on, Poo, dinnertime,' Padgett came along in some bewilderment, and eventually, as such men must, he asked. 'It's just that there's other words,' Lowndes said, and suggested three or four. Next day Padgett announced his intent in more soldierly fashion, and in utter silence every man laid down his tool, cigar, checker, ramrod, plug, pamphlet, pen, and Carlsbach said gently, 'The word is "poo", Padgett.' Padgett accepted his doom.

Haller too accepted his doom. He marched to the colour line like a sergeant, but today he glanced up and rubbed his hands; the sky was opaque, hostile, and there would be no respite, no warming gleam. Men stamped and flapped, breath misting thickly. Haller called the roll from memory. Catto, tapping his boot with a stout stick, a coil of rope in his left hand, strolled down to the sergeant and took his report. 'Last time,' Haller said.

'You'll have them back fast as I can work it,' Catto said, 'but as of now you're a private. No breakfast either. And no visitors. Go bundle up.'

'I got no warm mittens.'

'Silliman has. Just thank God for Silliman's mother. Go on. Be back here in five minutes.' He turned to the men: 'Dismiss. Go eat.'

Catto waited in the iron cold. He stood, calm, unhappy, listening to the crackle of the hairs in his nose at each breath, hearing also the shouts and clatter of an army at dawn. Unhappy, yes, and yet happy: this was his kingdom. He was a resident and not a visitor, and he felt proprietary about the camp; about the barracks, the weapons, the horses and mules, the men themselves. Hooker for a father! The company cook for a mother!

'All right,' Haller said. 'Let's have it done with.'

'Noon sharp.'

'Noon sharp.' Haller sat upon the frozen ground, his knees together and drawn up. There was not much to be seen of him: beneath his cap a scarf covered his ears and forehead; he bowed his head and huddled, and the collar of his greatcoat hid most of his face. Silliman's dark blue mittens covered his hands, and he seemed to be wearing several pairs of socks. Catto smiled unseen. The survivor. The scavenger and survivor, the pack rat.

Catto passed the long stick under Haller's knees; Haller hunched, docile, resigned, and thrust his arms forward beneath the stick, and joined his hands on his shins. Catto tied his wrists together tightly. Haller flapped his elbows an inch; the stick held them down. 'You're bucked,' Catto said. He produced a smaller stick, six inches long and an inch in diameter. Haller opened his mouth and Catto laid the stick across it; Haller's yellow teeth bit down on the wood. Catto bound twine to one end, passed it behind Haller's neck, bound it to the other end. 'You're gagged.'

Haller grunted.

'Don't bitch this up,' Catto said. 'Just sit tight for six hours. Going to be all sort of people passing by, and some of them going right back to Hooker and tell him what's what. If you fall sideways just lie there. I'll check in every half-hour. Whisky in my shack after the noonday meal.'

Haller tried to smile, but settled for bright eyes and greedy nodding.

By ten the tip of Haller's nose was blue. He shivered, long shudders, racking. 'Ah God,' Catto said aloud. Across the wind-swept drill ground a troop of horsemen reined in; two hundred yards, Catto estimated, aiming instinctively, and wondered who they were, but could not tell. 'Two hours,' he said. 'Can you do it?' Haller nodded. 'Back soon,' Catto said. Haller blinked.

Catto found his men ('I have to go look for them,' he had complained to Silliman. 'They don't really belong here. My orphans were better men') badgering the company cook about one thing and another, jests and jibes and many a laugh. He called them to attention savagely. They milled. Routledge was lost in conversation with a mule driver, a man bundled up to the hair, and a wool hat on top of the bundle. Hardly a human being at all. The mule stood glum, steaming. Routledge and the man turned, and Catto recognized Thomas Martin. He warmed for a moment: 'Hey boy!' Martin waved and grinned. Routledge had tottered around to inspect the mule's teeth ('It's the urge to be an authority,' Phelan said later. 'The supreme moment of a country boy's intellectual life') and was soothing the beast with strokes along the muzzle. Catto knew, absolutely; he maintained to the end of his life that something – God, the signs of the zodiac, instinct, or an utter and perfect communion with earth, air, fire, water and other essential atomies – had told him, given a second, two seconds, of clear, unmistakable warning; and he told this story for almost sixty years because he saw, in his life, prodigies of evil and prodigies of good but only one prodigy that was simply a prodigy, a violation for its own sake of all natural law, expectation, probability and philosophical or biological principle – Catto knew, then, that the rules were about to be suspended, and in those two seconds he forgot about Haller, and the war, forgot the entire existing universe save Routledge and that mule. He had faith.

And was rewarded. He was the only man to see it. Routledge was standing directly in front of the mule, stroking its muzzle, crooning and kissing, and the mule knocked him down *with a hind foot.* Like lightning. And was instantly his old feeble-minded unmoving self. Routledge got up slowly, with the look on his face of a man who has seen God; he stared at the mule and at Thomas Martin and straight up for a time. Then he shrank. He shrivelled visibly, walked over to Catto, his eyes pleading up from the bottom of a deep, dark well of misfortune, and said, 'You got to get me out of the army, Lieutenant.'

'You bet your ass,' Catto said with feeling.

He marched them to the company area and made a speech. 'I mean what I said: nobody's to touch Haller or talk to him. But I want you all out there, close by the colour line, ten or a dozen at a time anyway while the rest get warm. Just talk and make jokes. You all owe him something. Some of you your heads. And where do I find you? Clowning it with the cook, looking to get hot coffee I suppose. Sons of bitches.' For a moment he was shaken; his voice blazed. 'Go on out there. Godwinson, you're my sergeant now. It's official. Have a couple of men bring that chest.'

Catto paced near Haller in the yellow cold, the wind congealing him, turning Haller to stone. Silliman joined them. Haller nodded, blue. The chest was brought. The men lined up, sheepish, with their squares of cloth or oilskin pouches or silken bags. Haller watched while Godwinson quickly distributed several pounds of coffee, and several pounds of sugar, and some tea; twenty-two small candles, seventeen bars of yellow soap. 'What do we do with these boots, Lieutenant?'

'Find the four men with the dirtiest feet,' Catto snarled. 'Now haul that stuff out of here and come back to keep the man company.' He noticed then another small troop of horsemen, far across the drill field, the wind sawing down between him and them like a river; they seemed to tremble. 'Spies,' he muttered. Silliman said, 'More than that. You just look close.'

So Catto saw the blue eyes, or thought he did, that far off, and stood fast until the troop trotted close, and noticed again the incipient double chin, noticed it this time with surly satisfaction. They trotted nearer. Hooker inspected Haller with a deliberate and obvious cock of the head. Then they were within saluting range. Catto and Silliman did the correct thing. Catto stood once more like a wooden soldier, eyes front, immobile (but his teeth were set, and he ached), and gathered in Hooker's image only for a brief space, the plumed hat, the blue eyes, the rosy cheeks, the – by God! – broad smile, and then the general kicked his racy grey into a canter and Catto turned his back.

By noon Haller was almost unconscious. Catto and Silliman carried him into their shack, laid him down, rubbed his limbs. Godwinson ran for Phelan. Phelan ordered Haller to the infirmary, and Catto told him all about it.

'Hooker is a strange man,' Phelan said. 'Do you know he told the surgeons he would like to be remembered for the best military hospitals in the whole Union army? He *knows* things. He gives orders. He wants bromine used for gas gangrene and he says sodium hypochlorite is as good as carbolic. He personally forbids leeching. He inspects. He spends time with the sick. And then he does something like this. Ah, well. The human race is a great mistake.'

'I liked him when I met him. You know how you like some people right away. Now I think he is a savage. Or maybe touched.'

'No.' Phelan thought it over. 'He's a bad general in the fighting, and when things go wrong, but a good one otherwise. I heard the eastern armies were swimming in their own sewage before he came along. Beans killing more than bullets. He cleaned them up.'

'Good. Tell Haller.'

A day later Phelan poked his homely face into Catto's shack. 'Well, boy. And guess who spent an hour with Haller this morning.'

Catto sat there with his mouth open.

'I'm sorry,' said General August Willich on McLean Street in Cincinnati. 'I will try again, yes. But it is not the army way. When the war ends your man can go home.'

'Sir,' said Catto, and saluted, faced about, marched off, deciding that generals bored him considerably. He met the boy outside. 'Well. You again. How goes it?'

'Just fine.' The boy was always smiling, it seemed. Bearishly Catto wondered what the hell he had to smile about. 'Better'n freezing to death in Kentucky,' the boy went on. 'This is some winter, ain't it? A ball-buster.'

'In Kentucky too, I hear.'

'It's only across the river.'

'As I know to my sorrow. Tell me something. Been meaning to ask but I don't see you much. What happened to that rifle of your father's?'

The boy ganced at Catto's shoulder.

'Never mind that,' Catto said in mock anger. 'You got to stop remembering that bad shot. You ought to be ashamed, not proud.'

The boy laughed and said, 'General Willich's got it. When I go home I get it back. Pouch and horn too.'

'Good. You keep an eye on all that. We got some furacious soldiers around here.'

70

'Yeh?' The boy was plainly upset. 'What's that mean?'

'Thieves. All shapes and sizes. If I were you I'd plan to move out of here and go on home the very day the war ends. Don't hang about. We'll have a hundred men a day leaving Cincinnati with anything not nailed down.'

'I don't suppose they'd rob the general,' Thomas Martin said.

'They'd rob Lincoln. And that's a fine rifle. You mind what I say.'

'It may be you think more of that rifle than most,' the boy said.

'Don't sass. Want to walk along a bit?'

'Can't. Got to report, and then bring Jacob a sweater.'

'Haven't seen Jacob. How is he?'

'He's fine. Said he saw you many times.'

'Maybe he did. You take care now.'

'I'm sorry,' Catto said. 'There's still hope, but not much.'

Routledge fell back on his bunk, coughed harshly, and seemed to settle like a bad pudding. He was pale and unclean, a prisoner in a cold season; his presence rose to Catto's nostrils.

When it was certain that Routledge had nothing to say and could not be comforted, Catto left him. 'You better humour me, Ned. I'm about to declare war on the army. My God, man, what a prehistoric organization!'

'That's a disgraceful thing to say. You take their money.'

Catto had an excuse to curse, but refrained. 'Silliman, you're a nice boy,' was all he said.

The ladies sipped wine, the gentlemen gulped whisky, a waiter called Curly hovered. Bloodless Stanley in another part of the house greeted and smiled. Phelan's Nell was coloured like Catto: a healthy reddish tone to her, nothing scarlet or even pink, but a summery, fleshy rubescence like a cherry just turned. Dark yellow hair like silky autumn grasses. A bit older than Charlotte, who was twenty-seven, and a bit skinnier. Catto preferred his Cleopatra with the unpronounceable last name. Greek, he had thought. 'French,' she said.

Now Phelan was saying lazily, 'Something of interest in the doorway.'

Catto was replete: venison, potatoes, much beer, pie, coffee. He swigged once more at the tumbler and only then asked, 'What?' Nell and Charlotte had seen, and oohed, but Catto would not turn.

'A gentleman of importance.'

'You don't mean it,' Catto murmured, tightening. 'Alone?'

'A captain with him.'

'Tall, blond, no lips?'

'That's the fellow.' Phelan feigned respect. 'You seem to know just everybody, Lieutenant.'

'Dunglas. An aide, or a pimp, or something like that.'

Silence settled upon the table. Nell and Charlotte turned pale and furious; Phelan shot Catto a glance of pain, anger and contempt. Oh God damn me for that word, Catto thought, near to tears. Oh Jesus cut out my tongue. He closed his eyes. Rats gnawed his heart. Grow up, grow up, grow up! You have killed!

'Perhaps he will stop by and favour us with conversation,' Phelan said lightly.

Catto turned to Charlotte, who sat regarding her wineglass. He looked at Nell, who would not meet his eye. Phelan emanated courteous despair.

As his heart broke, because we are all such sad creatures, Catto reached for Charlotte's hand; she let him take it; he carried it to his lips and gently, gravely kissed it. She squeezed his fingers and smiled sadly.

'We shall have to order you some knee-breeches,' Phelan said softly, and Nell laughed a warm pardon.

'And what is the general doing now?' He did not release Charlotte's hand.

'Well, he's moving this way,' Phelan said with brisk interest. The saloon seemed to dim briefly as talk and laughter thinned. 'Shall we notice him?'

Charlotte reclaimed her hand and touched her hair.

'Only if he notices us,' Catto said. 'Common decency. Don't want to spoil the man's evening.'

Then he saw Phelan rise, and he glanced up with interest but no haste. 'General Hooker, sir,' he said affably, and reared up slowly, blinking, a half-smile on his face, altogether the well-born client greeting a rich grocer.

Hooker shouted laughter; heads turned. 'By God, boy,' he crowed, 'you'll do. And you, Surgeon: keep an eye on this young fellow. Damned if he doesn't run the whole show some-day. And you, Catto: be careful. With another general you'd have been over the line long ago.'

'Yes sir,' Catto said quickly. 'May I present Miss Charlotte and Miss Nell. General Hooker and Captain Douglas.'

'Dunglas,' said Dunglas, and smiled, bowing slightly. Hooker was inspecting the ladies, friendly yet aloof, some hint of the grand manner to him; he smelled of whisky, and with the whisky, Catto thought, a musky sort of tired-rakehell lechery, like a great lover trying to accomplish his possible before the buttocks went stringy or the teeth brown. 'How do you do, ladies.'

The ladies returned his salutation with gracious curtsies of the head and a glimpse of gum. Catto saw how nervous they were, and suppressed a laugh.

'I must say, Dunglas,' Hooker observed, 'that the level of manners in this country is rising fast. Not only these charming ladies smiling at me; even lieutenants stand up at my approach. Tell you what, Catto.'

Catto fell serious; there was that in the general's voice. He straightened. 'Sir.'

'You keep at it,' Hooker said roughly. 'Never lose faith in the army. Even when the politicians come meddling. You keep at it, hear me? You're the right sort, boy.'

'Thank you, sir. I, ah – '

'What is it?'

Catto was resisting affection. This was Hooker, fifty years old, a libertine, bad tactician, maker of excuses and not vic-tories, hothead, martinet; not a tender and reliable old gaffer to be cherished. But Catto liked him (or was it envy? or fear? Damn!) and for a moment could not speak, torn between his pleasure and his confusion. And Phelan probably grinning in-side!

Sharply Catto expelled a deep breath. 'I'd like those stripes back, sir.'

Hooker murmured, 'You would, would you?' They were silent. 'We seem to be attracting attention. Come along, Dunglas. Ladies. Gentlemen. Ah: Surgeon Phelan.'

'Sir.'

'I notice calomel and tartar emetic at the hospital.'

'Yes sir.'

'Do you approve?'

'No sir.'

'Then . . . '

'I couldn't say, sir.'

'I see. Surgeon Andrus. Well, he's leaving us.'

'He's a very good surgeon, sir.'

'Yes. He is. And knows nothing about food or medicine or cleanliness. I know the kind. I saw what they did to Hammond and Letterman.'

'Yes sir.'

'Anyway he's leaving,' Hooker said wearily. 'I may have some good news for you shortly.'

'Thank you, sir.'

'Good night to you all.' He led his aide away.

Catto and Phelan sat down. Phelan said to Nell, 'You see. Important men, we are.'

'All the same,' Catto said, 'there's a shine in your eyes. They glitter like gold leaves.'

'Go to the devil,' Phelan said, with a monstrous cheerful grin.

Catto reached for his cigar, and was as astonished as any of them at the tremulous flutter of his dancing hand.

Behind the screen, in their sleazy, glorious, partitioned loving room, Phelan lowed and clucked, proposed and ratified, flattered, nuzzled, discovered, invented, made public moan, boasted. Nell twittered and shifted. Catto was less hurried now. For a time he and Charlotte sat side by side like children, holding hands. The single lamp cast an eerie glow, reinforced by a January moon above the groves, pale and cold at the window; trapped between two friendly fires Charlotte gleamed, and was a girl again. Catto kissed her, unhurried, again, again, her own moons and groves. Whatever weary habit she had dragged to that room vanished, defeated or disguised. 'You're *funny*,' she said. He roamed her again. 'Oh God,' she said. Slowly she bore him away on witches' wings. Why, he wondered, do we bother with anything else? He smiled gratefully into the night. Slept in peace. Woke with the sun high, and turned away from her sour breath, and rose and washed, and brushed his teeth with whisky, and wanted to weep.

Otherwise it was a dull life. About a week later Haller came trudging up to him in evident despair. 'You got to help me again, Lieutenant.'

'Haller. How's your nose?'

'That's all right. I got a skin like leather anyway. It's no worse than a bad bruise now. The worst was those headaches. That night and all the next day.'

'What did Hooker talk about?' Catto felt excessively casual as he asked, like a spy perhaps.

'Mexico. And he wanted me to know why he done it to me.' Haller snorted, and cursed with no real anger. 'He was just making himself feel better. Everybody's papa.' He cursed more imaginatively.

'Did he mention Silliman or me?'

'No. But never mind him. Now look here, Lieutenant.'

'Yeh. You need help. What is it now?'

'Got a minute?'

They walked together to the barracks and marched inside, and Godwinson shouted the men to attention, and Catto told them to carry on. He followed Haller down the aisle, past the stove, his heart sinking at this new trouble, it could be nothing else, and at Haller's bunk the old private bent, grunting and wheezing as he dragged out that same chest. Haller flung it open and Catto saw several pounds of coffee, and several pounds of sugar, and some tea; twenty-two small candles, seventeen bars of yellow soap, and four pairs of brand-new boots size nine.

'It was nice of them,' Haller said, 'but next time that son of a bitch will shoot me.'

Chapter Five

'I ain't fooling,' the boy said. 'It hurts terrible.' His face was chalky, the eyes like blue moons. As he doubled up Catto winced with him, gasped with him.

'We better do something. Jacob, go see if you can find Phelan.'

Jacob fretted, wagging his head: 'He been like this all day. Maybe this March thaw got him upset.'

'You go fetch the surgeon.'

Jacob patted the boy in passing. 'You trust in God, now.' Thomas tried to smile.

'For God's sake, lie down,' Catto said. Thomas dragged himself to the cot and fell supine. Catto groaned wearily, hiked to the door and slammed it shut. 'This damn door. This damn army. This damn winter.'

'Oh be quiet,' Silliman said. 'Thomas, do you want a drink?'

'No.'

'Do you know what it is, Ned? Any idea at all?'

Silliman nodded. 'Side pleurisy. An aunt of mine – an aunt of mine had it.'

'Died of it,' he had been about to say, and Catto knew it. Catto had been depressed for some weeks, bored beyond endurance, and now he was trapped between fear for Thomas and a natural interest in whatever relieved the monotony. He woke with great reluctance these mornings, rising through layers of gum and bog towards an unnecessarily bright day, barking and swearing and spitting. He drank too much and Silliman worried.

'She had three attacks,' Silliman said.

'I had this once before,' Thomas said slowly, dreamily. 'About a year ago.'

Catto fidgeted and remembered the good old days, the days

of wrath and battle. He was tired now, sodden, red about the
eyes, yellow about the teeth, staled by cigars, unbathed. Very
different from this boy whose pale skin, unweathered, gleamed
smooth and white. The fair hair, dishevelled now, fell silky to
the blanket; the boy's ears were small, white, almost trans-
lucent; his nose was young, without character. Catto – thick-set,
moustachioed, hair in his nostrils, a leader of men – grew sadly
aware that his own boyhood was gone. Once, and not long ago,
his face too had been bland and open and innocent. 'Phelan will
make you well,' he said gently. 'Phelan is one of these professors. He knows everything. Willich will give you a week off.'

'Gen'l Willich.' There was rebuke in the boy's exhausted
voice, and Catto rather liked him for it; but in the next few
seconds that rebuke drifted between them like a mist upon the
water, curling slowly about an unkempt Catto, licking at a
heap of laundry, wisping silently to a whisky bottle half full, to
the officer's unshaven face, perforated sock, dried sweats.

'Gen'l Willich,' Catto conceded. 'What did your folks do for
it?'

'My mother's dead,' the boy said, 'and my pappy was drunk.
It just went away after a little.'

'Have you been out in the cold?' Silliman asked. 'Had the
sniffles or anything?'

'No. Nothing like that.'

'Just lie still,' Silliman said. 'You'll be all right.' But he
showed Catto a face of doubt and despair.

Phelan blew up. 'Side pleurisy? *Side pleurisy?* Get me a canteen full of cold water. Unless there's ice somewhere. Quick
now, Jacob. What damn barber called it side pleurisy?' His
moustache and brows danced, his eyes gleamed ferociously.

'It was a little fellow,' Silliman said, 'name of Doctor Simon
Howard.' He added apologetically 'He was very good with
chickens too, and animals generally.'

'For Christ's sake chickens!' Phelan roared. 'A barnyard man,
was he?'

'No, no,' Silliman said, placating, 'a real doctor. Good with
babies too, and broken bones. He used a stethoscope like yours.'

'That's better,' Phelan said. 'A surgeon in the Eighty-ninth told me Harvard hasn't even got one of those yet. But your little man is a damn fool anyway. Now you lie still,' he said to Thomas. 'I'm going to poke here and there. You tell me what it feels like.'

'Yahaaaow!'

'Is that right.'

'My God,' Catto said. 'Look at the sweat on him. In the wink of an eye like that.'

'Don't do it again,' Thomas whispered. 'Please.'

'Don't have to,' Phelan said. 'We know all we need to know. One thing more: you feel like vomiting?'

'Sometimes. Comes and goes.'

'That's it then. Pain's in the right place, your belly's like a board, you're a little warm. You're going into the hospital.'

Jacob pushed into the cabin waving a canteen. 'No more ice. Maybe in the morning with a good frost tonight. Here now, young Thomas. You drink this.'

'Drink hell,' Phelan said. 'Lay it on his belly. Give it here. Then fetch an ambulance. That feel cold? Good. Put him aboard and take him into town to the hospital, fast as you can. I'll ride in and meet you there.'

Catto huddled against the wind. He and Jacob wore identical greatcoats and blue wool stocking-caps. A cold sun mocked them. Jacob handled the reins with authority and the mule clopped along briskly as if in a hurry to be stabled. 'Be ye not as the horse or the mule, which have no understanding,' Jacob said suddenly. His eyes teared; he blinked away the cold. 'That's a wind. You know, I never been sick a day in my life.'

Beside him on the board Catto said, 'How long has that been?'

'Don't know for sure. More than forty but not yet forty-five.'

Catto looked him over. A man always showed better doing work he knew well. Jacob seemed taller. 'Where you from anyway, Jacob?'

'Tennessee.'

'How'd you get free?'

'When Mister Lincoln's men come by, I just run off and jine with them. You don't remember, do you.'

'Remember?'

'You one of the first soldiers I see. I still remember. You remember that bright red horse you had? Little fellow. Pony, like.'

'The roan. Sure I remember him.' Catto smiled his astonishment, then bowed his head and concentrated. Jacob had said, 'You one d'fust sojas ah see. Ah stee memba. You memba dah brah reh hoas you ha? Lil fella. Pony lak.' But Catto had heard speech, all clear and simple. Did he sound as odd to Jacob, and yet as natural? Interesting. Puzzling. Like maybe a trip to China and some little yellow man eating with a pair of wooden sticks, but he was eating beef and rice and chicken and when he was all finished he looked up and said, 'Not bad, Marius. Have some,' and in an odd way you might as well be in Illinois. 'And you remember me from back then,' said Catto the traveller. 'I was a sergeant then.'

'That's right,' Jacob said with satisfaction.

'Well I'll be,' Catto said. 'Well I'll be. You know, that was the last time I had a horse. I stole him and I only had him three days. He was a frisky little fellow.'

Catto fell into a reverie as they jolted along; he swayed, clung, remembered. Chickamauga. He loved the name itself: Chickamauga! One moment there he would never forget, a moment in the morning, himself high above a valley, above a mountain pass, sitting the roan and bewildered at the distant swell of sound, seeing an advance guard enter the pass, and then the main body, far below, a long line of blue against the greens and yellows and reds and browns of autumn, and soon there were thousands of them, the sun flashing on buckles and bayonets, and the morning air carried that swell of sound, and he understood: they were singing; high above those thousands he heard the chorus, as if they sang for him alone. *Mine eyes have seen the glory of the coming of the Lord*; the words unfurled over half of Tennessee, and Catto was happy to be alone because there was no holding back a tear or two. Then he rejoined his unit and a drunken fool named Biddle was singing the same tune but other words, and the men chimed in:

When the war is over we will all enlist again,
When the war is over we will all enlist again,
When the war is over we will all enlist again,
We will, like hell we will!

'Then you've been a free man for quite a while,' he said to Jacob.

'Year and a half,' Jacob said. 'That's not long.'

'I see what you mean. But you haven't been with this regiment all that time.'

'No sir. Been with several.'

'By golly,' Catto said. 'We're old friends. Old friends from Chickamauga.'

'Yes sir.'

'What's your last name?'

'Courtney.'

'Courtney. That's a fine old name.'

'My pappy's master's name. So they told me. I never see my pappy. Or my mammy.'

'Well, me too, in a way,' Catto said awkwardly. 'But it's not the same. I heard about things like that, families all scattered.'

After a pause he plunged on: 'When you ran off, did you – oh hell. Never mind.'

'You ask me anything you like. I never did evil.'

'Well, that's what I wondered. If you'd killed anyone, or fired a house.'

'No, no, no. Just run off. Not but what I would have *liked* to, maybe. But between liking and doing there stands the Lord.'

'You sound like a Bible reader.'

'I am. I am that.' The wagon trundled through ruts, jolting them together.

'Easy,' Catto said. 'The boy.'

'Doing as best I can.'

'Where'd you learn to read?'

'Funny thing,' Jacob said. 'For about five years, some time back, a crazy little white lady from Connetic set up with Bibles nearby where I live. And about six or seven black folks learn their letters and how to read the Good Book. And then the masters run the lady off, they say some awful things about her, but you know I bet we got twenty, twenty-five niggers can read nearby where I live, from those first six or seven. And the word is a lamp unto my feet and a light unto my path.'

'Well, that's fine,' Catto said. 'I don't believe Thomas can read.'

'Well, the boy a Catholic. He don't have to read. He have the priests read for him.' Jacob's tone was not merely explanatory; it was kind.

'Is that right.' Catto choked back laughter, laughter not at Jacob but at Phelan, at Phelan's face when he heard. Then he thought ruefully, I could have been a colonel. I do believe saying no was stupid.

Gently, silently, he sniffed. Nothing. Stiff breeze, and Jacob in wool. Still, at this range Franklin could kill. And old Catto is not so savoury these days either. 'What do you know about the boy?'

'He's a good boy.'

'I know he's a good boy. What about his family? His home?'

'Not much of that,' Jacob said. 'You know about his father. Drunk all the time. Boy's mother died a long time ago. She had to keep to her bed and she hurt bad, hurt bad for many months. The boy almost cry when he tell me that.'

Catto fell glum. Was the boy lucky to have had a mother even if he had to lose her? a father even if a drunkard? Who was luckier, Thomas or Marius?

'So the boy always pretty much alone,' Jacob went on. 'Live off what he hunt, and keep to the woods a lot. He don't even know what this war all about.'

'Neither do I, some days.'

'About slavery, this war is. No doubt about that. About Jacob Courtney and his people.' Jacob's voice lost assurance: 'Lieutenant, sir, they going to make the boy all right, ain't they?'

'Don't you fret. Phelan is the best.'

'That's good. I'll send up a prayer.' He pointed: 'We almost there now.'

'What will you do to him?' The noontime air nipped, the sky was frosty blue; Catto's cheeks burned. 'I ought to be bled. I

6

feel like I had about a gallon too much of the vital juices.'

'It is youth and lust,' Phelan said. 'Side pleurisy! There is no such bloody thing as side pleurisy, and even good doctors are fools at times.'

'Then what will you do?'

'Open him up,' Phelan said, 'and take out a useless bit as long as your little finger, namely the appendix. Side pleurisy!'

'Open him up,' Catto murmured, and was cold with fear.

'Cheer up,' said Phelan. '*Omnia mors aequat.*'

'If you must swoon or retch, please leave the operating room,' Phelan said. They were walking a grey corridor, Phelan all brisk and commanding, no lubricious smiles, no elfin wagglings, Catto reluctant, lumbering and lowering. 'I don't want you too close, either.'

Catto reflected that he had never broken a bone or lost a limb; he wondered if his fingers and toes counted as limbs. 'I could pass this by,' he said, 'but it's the boy. Seems like I owe it to him to be there.'

'Well and nobly spoken,' Phelan said, and laughed aloud, eager, paying little mind really to Catto. 'I've never done this before.' Left, right, left, right, they marched, and their heels came down hard on the wooden floor; Catto felt, with pleasure, the slight jar along his spine at each pounding step. 'But I've seen it done. Nothing to it.'

Catto was silent. He felt a frippery and superfluous fellow, necessary to no one. He repeated to himself that there was no difference between blood spilled on a battlefield and blood spilled on a table; between Garesche's drenching Rosecrans and the boy's oozing into a swab. But he could not believe that. The difference between a clean, accidental wound, even in the belly, and a deliberate incision (in the belly!) mystified him. Then he was ashamed and said, 'Anything I can do, you tell me. Carry out the garbage, anything.'

'No, no. We have orderlies for that. Black fellows. Do you know what garbage means in the old country?'

'No.' Nor cared, right now.

'Wheats and straws all chopped fine to feed the horses.'

'Is that right.'

'Cheer up, boy. You won't be able to see much.'

'That's just as well. I thought you didn't like black fellows.'

'No, I don't,' Phelan said. 'But they do dirty work with no complaints. And . . . '

'And what?'

'Well, don't talk about this, but the white orderlies have a tendency to steal morphine and sell it. The blacks don't.'

'Will you use that on Thomas?'

'No. Just chloroform. I tell you, that's the part that scares me. You can kill a man putting him to sleep. I wish I knew more about it.'

They climbed to the second storey. In the hall sat the inevitable iron stove and the inevitable clerk, a fat corporal in serious need of a shave, a wash, a trim and a handkerchief. 'Af'noon, doc,' said this Gabriel. Phelan nodded and breezed by; the corporal's eyes quizzed Catto, who stared him down and followed Phelan. They paced in single file through a long ward, and Catto, somewhat embarrassed and not sure why, uneasy and flushed, tried not to notice bandages, empty trouser-legs, urinals in use. He passed the recreation table, saw playing cards, a cribbage board, an almanac; its cover caught his eye and he paused, furtive: an opulent milkmaid, spilling out of stockings and bodice, stared boldly out at dear reader with vacant shining eye and pendulous avid lip, the soldier's eternal succubus. Catto blinked and reached for an open book prone upon the table: *David Copperfield*. He dropped it and hastened after Phelan.

Phelan was surveying a bright room about twenty feet by fifteen. He pointed to a chair and spoke, not to his old comrade Catto but to a fool and potential nuisance who must be made to understand. 'You sit there. And stay put unless – like I said. Then get out fast. If you feel all right you can stand up to see better, but don't move about.' Catto nodded and sat down. Phelan puttered about the tables that lined two walls, muttering to his knives and his clamps, his needles and his thread. 'Carbolic,' he said once, to no one. Then he stepped through the doorway and abandoned Catto among unfamiliar devices, glittering about him like gew-gaws and baubles, impressive yet frightening. Catto removed his hat, flapped it tentatively at possible resting places, then restored it to its accustomed perch. His mind saw a razory scalpel gashing a livid paunch. Blood welled in drops, then runnels, then rivers. Assorted globular bladders emerged; pink sausages, burgundy livers. Various minute creatures peered up from the incision, indignant: the little people, gods of digestion – Catto blinked. He found a door, then a window, and fresh air. When the fit had passed he went to find Thomas.

The boy lay in a long room among other patients. Jacob hovered. Catto nodded once at the others, carefully overlooking the details of their misery, and carried a wooden chair to the boy's bedside. 'Phelan tells me you'll be fine.'

'It's scary. They shaved me.' Thomas blushed.

'It's always scary, I suppose. You scared hell out of me once.'

Thomas smiled weakly.

'You're a fine boy,' Catto said. 'You'll do. What were you before all this anyway? Farmer? Schoolboy?'

'Farmer. Never went to school. But the farm was no use without pa and he was mostly drunk. When he was sober he hunted.'

'With that rifle.'

'With that rifle.'

'A better shot than you.'

'He was, when he was sober.'

'How'd you come to have the rifle?'

Thomas hesitated for the space of several breaths. With the rough sheet Catto sponged sweat from the boy's face. Gently Jacob stayed him, and with a moist towel supplanted him. 'Well, I run off,' Thomas said. 'He was laying somewhere, I reckon, not too far from a barrel of whisky. I wanted to be a soldier. And I heard they had no guns. No nothing. Colonel Jessee was my hero and he was passing through so I grabbed the rifle and . . . ' He panted briefly. 'Oh it hurts. Oh Lieutenant.'

'You hang on,' Catto said softly. 'I'll go tell them to hurry.'

'Yeh. Yeh. Hurry.'

With a quick nod to Jacob, Catto returned to the operating room. It was empty but shortly Phelan came bustling in to find him. 'We're almost ready. In or out?'

'In,' said Catto. 'The boy hurts. Hurry it up.' Again he saw blood, swelling veins like pink worms, shiny white bone. He swallowed vigorously. A man had followed Phelan into the small room. 'Surgeon Shadbolt,' Phelan said, 'Lieutenant Catto.' Catto and the surgeon shook hands; Shadbolt was older, near fifty, and Catto was unaccountably comforted. Shadbolt had white hair and the look of a saint: light blue eyes, weary, and a sad smile. 'Don't worry,' the saint said. 'I've done this before.'

'I'm glad to hear it, sir,' Catto said most courteously. 'I hope you'll tell the boy. It would cheer him up.'

'I will, then.' Shadbolt excused himself and inspected his ranked instruments. Catto craned to see: this was like the shelves and bins of a hardware shop, and he felt some of the excitement he had always felt before boxes of bits and barrels of nails, sheaves of rasps, trays and jars and pigeon-holes full of clamps, screws, nuts, bolts, cotter-pins; balls of twine and lead weights, hide-scrapers and penknives, wicks and candles and oil-lamps, hammers and awls. The memory of a general store in Illinois came to him, and of his first penknife, quickly stolen by parties unknown. But he was roused by the step of a third medical person, an orderly, a young man sallow and gloomy, a mulatto perhaps, not smocked like the doctors but dressed for sweeping and scrubbing, like the caretaker of a town hall. No name; he and Catto nodded. The young man then lit several small lamps and turned them high, and set them on shelves and tables. The room was suddenly bright, the windows pale. Phelan pointed to one: 'We'd better have that open a bit.' The orderly complied. With soft swearing and the shrieks of tortured wood two more orderlies pushed an awkward wheeled bed into the room: upon it lay Thomas, frail beneath a sheet. He saw Catto and tried to smile. 'Lieutenant.'

'Thomas. How is it now?'

'The same. I'm scared.'

'Well don't be,' Catto and Phelan said in chorus.

'Nothing will go wrong,' Phelan said. 'You're a strong healthy boy and you'll be fine.'

'My father.'

'What about him?'

'If – '

'If,' Catto said. 'Thomas, don't you worry.'

The boy's face crumpled but he said, 'All right. If you say so.'

'My name is Shadbolt.' The old man smiled down; Thomas grinned, a ghastly rictus. 'I've done this before. It isn't hard, and we're not going to lose you. I want you to know that.'

'Oh, I know that,' Thomas said, 'I know that, I'll be all right,' and sobbed hopelessly, gushing sudden tears. Catto froze.

'Lie still and breathe easy,' Shadbolt said. The mask covered Thomas's face; watching him Catto gasped and suffocated slightly. Chloroform dripped. The patient's lungs pumped properly. His eyes closed. 'He's out,' said Shadbolt, and blew his nose, trumpeting into a red bandanna. 'I'll give him a bit longer,' said Phelan. They waited. 'Now,' Phelan decided. 'The sideways incision, as you said.'

'Yes. I don't know yet which is best. But it's doubtless better to cut with the grain.'

With the grain. Like a roast. Most of Thomas was beneath the sheet; Phelan worked on an anonymous patch of living skin. Catto made no effort to watch closely. He sniffed at the chloroform and was the worse for it. Shadbolt and Phelan muttered like witches. 'Yes. There. Swab it. Now a little wider. Good.' Catto withdrew, and drowsed. Thomas had said, 'Thanks for coming, Lieutenant.' His last words, perhaps. Catto wondered what his own last words would be. An angry oath, he hoped. And where was Jacob? The surgeons muttered more. Catto drifted, sweating slightly. Garesche. The headless horseman. That was a story. Mrs McIntyre read that story. The boys shivered and giggled. That night Catto woke weeping. 'Clamp now.' Catto blinked and stirred. He thought, as if it were his duty, of Thomas Martin. God let him live to be a man. A cheerful boy set down by fate among hazards and lightnings. A hard worker, and that streak of assurance. If he lived the world would lie open to him, this abundance, this Union preserved; he could go west, make a life, land, buffalo, travel, campfires, some day a wife and a house and the war forgotten, only a few memories of the time of trouble, and he would tell the story –

Shot an officer, I did, fellow name of Catto and where is he now.

The surgeons seemed purposeful, unflurried; they were men of courage and experience, were they not. The school of war. War! Catto's school too. Better battle than surgery. No more battles, though. Not now. Like Thomas he was free. This vast land. Months to cross. Alone. The boy would live. The boy must live. In all the world he owed only Catto, and that a small debt, nothing like a life, and anyway Catto had forgiven him. Debt discharged. And the war over and the farewells, and Catto on his way. Alone. The Rocky Mountains. Catto contracted invisibly, in a wrenching spasm of misanthropy: his vision cleared and he saw himself on horseback, alone, in a pine forest fringing the flank of a tall mountain; he proposed to make camp beside a clear, dancing mountain stream. There was no human being for a hundred miles; he was inordinately happy, and groaned aloud.

'Are you all right?' the voice was Phelan's.

'All right,' Catto said. He saw Phelan, and nodded.

Phelan grinned, turned swiftly, and with a quick gesture tossed something to Catto. Catto made the catch by instinct, but revulsion had already boiled through his blood and into his belly. He looked down, knowing, full of horror. Phelan said, 'You see why we call it vermiform.'

'I don't know what that means,' Catto started to say; the words were cut off by a babyish moment of pure and absolute helplessness, in turn cut off by the sudden and unaccountable levitation of the floor itself, which inspired Catto to clutch in panic at the arms of his chair; but his arms would not flex, and his hands would not seize, because he was fainting dead away.

Jacob found him next day, surprised him shaving after the morning roll call, sidled into the cabin and said, 'Thomas going to be all right. So they say.'

'You saw him?'

'Yes I did. And Cap'n Phelan too, up and about at sunrise, and Thomas weak like a baby but the Cap'n say everything look fine.'

'Well thank God for that. Thank God for that.'

'I did,' Jacob said, and then slyly, 'I hear you not so fine.'

'Now don't make fun of me. You wouldn't have been so fine either.'

'No, that's true. I didn't mean nothin' by it.'

Catto grinned. 'I have enough trouble with the boy making fun of me.'

Jacob laughed. 'A great one for fun, that boy. You know what he ask me to tell you? He and you all even now, that's what.'

Catto shared the chuckle, wide awake with relief. 'I can tell you now, I was scared.'

Jacob shook his head. 'No need to fear. Everybody say Cap'n Phelan the best. The best.'

'Haw. You had breakfast?'

'Just hot coffee.'

'Come on. Sit with me and Silliman and tell us all about it.' He paused, and squinted. 'I bet you were at the hospital all night.'

'That's right. But I slept in a bed. I like that.' Jacob smiled faintly. 'You know, sometimes I get tired. I'm not a boy no more. You working me too hard.'

By golly, Catto started to say, give a man his freedom and next thing he wants to be president; but something in him bit back the remark.

It was another Catto, the Catto of old, who trotted into Cincinnati on Saturday a week later. The boy was well and walking about, and Catto, in thanks and praise, had reformed somewhat. He rode erect and feared no man, dreaming now of Charlotte, now of pot roast. He seemed today to take for granted his horse, his bar, the occasional salute, the grudging envy of a wagoneer. The cold air conduced to pride, to a mysterious sort of good health, as if he were finally an officer not by virtue of trappings, of insignia, but by his own true virtue, by an inner transformation, so that he was now fully commissioned in his bath also, or in the bedchamber. He was on a street now, not a road, a city street hemmed by signs, FRESH MEATS DAILY BUTCHERING CIGARS AND SNUFF THE BANK OF SOUTHERN OHIO EBLING'S DRY GOODS THE RHEIN-

GARTEN, and his charger slowed from a jog. They made their stately way along the slippery cobblestones. Third Street. East Third Street. One hundred and nineteen East Third Street. Civilized. Catto approved. An elegant address, with a number and a knocker. Not even a sentry outside. He hitched his horse and promised to be quick, and let himself into one hundred and nineteen East Third Street.

'You won't say no to schnapps.'

'No, I won't, thank you, sir. That is, I won't say no.'

With his teeth Willich removed the cork; with his left hand he poured two ponies full. 'Drink up.' Catto stepped to the desk and took one glass, Willich raised the other and said something foreign; they sipped. 'Ah. It takes me back. I rarely touch it now but it takes me back.' The general smiled almost dreamily. He stood like a general, he did, with that ramrod back; Catto vowed to practise.

He sucked fumes. 'What is it, sir? It tastes like, like – '

'Like little cakes, or bread. Am I correct?'

'That's right.'

Willich told him what it was and Catto forgot immediately. Willich corked the bottle and set it aside. 'Sit down now. How is life?'

'Very dull, sir. Not like the good old days.'

'The good old days. For me the good old days is revolution, which is a different thing. With secret meetings and secret presses, and not so much guns.'

'Yes sir. It's been some time since we had that here.'

'Ach God,' Willich said, his voice weary and yearning, 'a new country like this.' He flapped a hand like a scornful haggler; the other hung limp. 'We had centuries of kings, emperors, princes, barons. Impossible to describe the damage. So all we had to work with was frightened farmers and a few professors. We were our own slaves, you see.'

Catto almost saw, and so nodded.

Willich breathed guttural disgust, dismay, nostalgia, 'Ach, ja, ach, ja,' and then cheered up: 'well, well, a bit at a time, hey?'

'Yes sir.'

'Yes. Now. This man of yours. This Routledge.'

Catto waited, incredulous.

'Over forty and not much good.'

'That's right, sir. We haven't much use for him.'

'Yes, yes. You see most of the soldiers in Cincinnati are Veterans Reserve Corps, so they all have something wrong with them – they are crippled like me or half blind. I have some from the Thirty-seventh Iowa and some from the Hundred Ninety-second Pennsylvania. They all want to go home. They all deserve to.'

Catto said something agreeable.

'And if Morgan wants to come up again and raid as he did in sixty-three, I must have troops nearby to chase him down. My boys here in the city could hardly do it. You see: to be ready. However. Just the same. I understood what you were telling me about this man, this Routledge. A Jonah, attracting the lightning of the gods to those around him.'

'Did I say that?'

'No.' Willich laughed lightly, a clear German spring, laughed with an accent. That's crazy, Catto thought. He remembered Phelan shouting 'Och, och' something like this German general. 'No, you did not say that. But I suppose it is true.'

'It is,' Catto said, and told him about the mule.

Willich roared. 'Impossible. Impossible.'

'I saw it.'

'After the war you must write it for my newspaper,' the general said. 'So. You see why we must offer him to the gods.'

'What does that mean?'

'That we find a way to send him home. It is possible that the gods are jealous of him, and want him for themselves. Once out of the army, he is theirs. Fair enough?'

Catto stammered.

'I have a certain discretion,' Willich went on. 'First I must attach him directly to my command here, to my legion of the deformed and mutilated. It is my private opinion that we ought to be sending men home now anyway. Otherwise the war will end and they will all have to go home at once, and there will be no transportation and then no jobs and half of them will go home sick and spread diseases and so on.' Willich rose. 'You may tell him. He will be transferred from your unit as soon as I can arrange it. Now I want you to come with me.'

'General, I don't know how to thank you.'

'You can help me with my coat for a start.' Willich smiled again, his fair, blond, white-toothed smile, the blue eyes warming. 'Generals have their uses. Thank you. Did you come mounted, or by wagon?'

'Mounted.'

'Good.' He opened the door and bellowed for his horse to be made ready. 'We'll wait in the hall here. March wind still blowing, I suppose.'

'That's right, sir.'

'Mmm. It's all right at night, with a good fire. I hope you're comfortably quartered out there.'

'Yes sir. Good tight wooden barracks and cabins. Do you live here, sir?'

'Here? McLean Barracks, you mean? Not on your life, boy. No. I stay in Mount Auburn, with Johann Stallo. Do you know Judge Stallo? You must meet him. A mathematician of note, also a physicist, and a pillar of the law. General Wallace invited him a couple of years ago to become a civilian judge advocate, a supreme court, you might say almost, for this district.'

Catto was saying 'Mm. Mm. Mm. Yessir,' wishing the general's horse would arrive, wondering where this day would take him, hoping for another hooker of that foreign liquor and impatient to see old Routledge. 'Routledge,' he would say, 'Routledge, my lad, I'm sorry, old son, but we're going to have to let you go. Things just haven't worked out. No hard feelings.'

The general and the lieutenant jogged cautiously, hunched and wrapped against the bitter winds. 'The River Rhine, way up there,' said Willich with a flourish of one gloved hand; the reins flapped. 'You know what we call that section there, to the north?'

'Over-the-Rhine.'

'Ah. You know the city then.'

'Some.'

'The Black Bear.'

Catto laughed. 'I've heard of it. Not been there.'

'Nor I,' Willich said, smiling. 'No carousing since I was a student,' he went on in mock grief, 'and not much even then. It is not good to be born into busy times. As you are discovering.'

'I don't mind.'

Willich was flagrantly a general and Catto was happy to be riding beside him. Wagons and carriages skirted them respectfully. Drivers saluted. Catto sat tall and gazed out at the world with cool, critical eyes and a severe set to his lips. After a long silence he wondered if Willich might be laughing at him.

'This is a sad city,' said the general. 'You know up there the police cannot even come. My own people. Honest peasants with a love of beer. Hm, hm. Half the taverns in the city are in a few blocks over that way, and half the brothels too. And fifty families in a building, with one privy.'

Catto was silent, and thought of Phelan.

'We try,' said Willich. 'You know before the war I published the *Deutsche Republikaner*. I tried to make them proud of themselves, proud to be German, also American. It made them so proud that they fought every day with the Irish or the black men. This country is worse than Europe in that – everyone belongs to a little club of his own people, and despises everyone else. You remember Morgan's raid in sixty-two?'

'I wasn't in the neighbourhood in sixty-two, sir.'

'That's right. Well, Morgan came up and jabbed at Lexington, so we sent troops down to help; and the city council, God bless them, all turned into generals and sent a hundred and twenty policemen with them, in the middle of serious riots right here.'

'Draft riots?'

'Nix, nix. The Irishers and the Negers. With the war we lost most of the shipping trade on the river, so there were not so many jobs for stevedores. So the Irishers tried to drive off the black men, declared war on them, invaded Bucktown, and so forth. They burned the Shakespeare House.'

'A theatre?'

Willich laughed. 'A bordello.'

'Who won the war?' Catto was slowly freezing; his cold eyelids drooped.

'The Irishers, I suppose. Anyway the Negers kept away from the waterfront after that. And you know my own people were mixed up in it too. Some said the Irishers were striking, and the Germans came to take their jobs but got scared off, and then the black men, who did not scare so easily.'

'A soldier's life is simpler.' Except for listening to generals. Where are we going? Should I ask?

'You see, I worry because I think this country is the last real chance on earth. If we can save this country then in time the others will follow us, and the world will be a great republic, with free men everywhere. You understand.'

'Well, I hope you're right, sir,' Catto said.

'Mm. Well. Of course there is a certain natural depravity in man that stands in the way.'

Oh my God.

'We have too many Wallensteins and not enough Schillers,' said this stately European.

Oh my God again.

'And why do I bother you with this,' the general wondered.

'It's very interesting,' Catto said.

'I tell it to you because you are so American. Everything. Your shape, your colour, your manner. Even your obvious ability to transcend ignorance.'

'Thank you, sir,' said Catto.

'Just remember. The last chance for decency. For charity and generosity and true brotherhood. *Alle menschen.*'

'Yes sir,' Catto said. '*Alle menschen.*' *Omnis morris.*

'And here we are,' said General Willich.

It was a grand house and suitable, as might be occupied by senators, magnates of the old blood, whisky wholesalers and other patricians; it lacked a lick of white paint but flaunted fluted pillars fencing a deep front porch patrolled now by a strapping sentry who saluted, sullen in the cold, and descended to take the reins. The officers clumped to the porch. Catto's boots were no longer bright; he buffed buttons, and followed Willich into the house.

Once in the drawing-room he quailed: a covey of generals and colonels, a few civilians, all ancient, bearded, grey. He stood to attention, but his mutinous eyes roamed; as he felt his heartbeat quicken he noted eight or nine officers, appropriate furniture, a major at a desk, writing with his back to Catto, three grave elders, a stone fireplace and the flicker and hiss of cheery flames, a patterned carpet, a sideboard, bottles, decanters, a piano against one wall and above it a life-sized painting in a scrolled gold frame of a fat woman, reclining, wearing a small sheet of paper. Her breasts were plump, her red mouth at once amused and voracious; he understood that the sheet of paper was a letter, and judged from its position and her amusement that it was a love letter. Did she come with the house? Whose house was this? Where am I and what are they doing to me?

'An amateur of the arts, I see.' It was Dunglas the dancing-master, gliding close to stare down with his ice-blue eyes.

'I just came along with General Willich.'

'So you did. I think you may stand at ease.'

Catto relaxed formally. 'Sir.'

'I'll remind the general. He won't want to keep you from your duties.'

'Fact is, I'm not too busy today. I could use a few minutes more with that lady.' Soldier-talk, he was suddenly, uncomfortably aware. In truth the lady was fatter than he liked.

Dunglas laughed and clapped him on the shoulder. All boys together. Perhaps Dunglas was not such a bad fellow. Catto saw Willich and Colonel Bardsley, and Hooker behind them, laughing out of that devilish, handsome, rakehell face. Pink cheeks; he kept out of the weather. Cold eyes like Dunglas; how did he choose his aides? A blade. The uniform spotless, unwrinkled. The general heard Dunglas, and beckoned to Catto, who strode forward, snappy, half fearful. Not fear, no. What then? He straightened and felt like a lackey, a poster, until Hooker said 'At ease, Catto' and order flowed back into the room, a comforting and reassuring order that regulated the universe, from

God to an ant, from Lincoln to Jacob, from Hooker to Catto. 'Make yourself at home for a moment, Catto. You know Colonel Bardsley, of course. Judge Dickson, Judge Stallo, Mister James Barnett there with the glass in his hand, something of a writer, you know; and General . . . ' But the generals were too much, and the names rattled by: General Hurly and General Burly and Colonels Fee, Fi, Fo and Fum. 'You'll have a drink, won't you?' Hooker asked, and Catto nodded and was still trying to squeeze out an elegant word of thanks when Hooker waved towards the assiduous, silent officer at the writing desk and said, 'Oh and of course you know Major Phelan.'

'Major Phelan?' Catto blurted the name and quality in tenor outrage as the writer turned, waggling fingers and twinkling, brows bouncing.

'Phelan,' Hooker said, ' a glass for Captain Catto.'

'Captain Catto?' He blurted that too, with the same outrage; they all laughed and he blushed and saw himself as he knew they must see him: naked, utterly hairless, uniformly pink. Beards wagged, rejoicing, approving. 'Sir,' he said shakily, and Phelan pressed a glass into his hand.

'You'd better drink that before you spill it on my carpet,' Hooker ordered merrily. 'We've already drunk to Major Phelan. This one is for you.'

'Yes sir.' Catto found to his surprise that he was capable of speech. 'I believe I could profit by it.'

'Bottoms up.'

Catto complied.

'Phelan will explain all this.'

'My compliments, Captain,' said Willich. 'Ah, I tell you, gentlemen, to be twenty-five once again.'

At that Catto experienced the first tickle of irritation, but he continued to smile while Phelan clapped him on the shoulder and chirped Hibernian nothings at him, begob this and me-lad that, and meanwhile the generals and colonels were buzzing and flapping and crowing. 'It's not much,' Hooker said, 'for a man who could have been a colonel at twenty-three,' and they gurgled and guffawed, and so did their buckles and eagles and stars and sabres and bright, bright boots, all winking and jiggling and chuckling. In a blinding and mournful moment Catto realized that he was sick of them, and one of them. But he was still grinning politely, and managed a fine, crisp, captainly salute, and turned about and left them, striding ahead of Phelan so that not even the great healer could see his burning eyes.

Thank God for cold air! He took it in like fire, like medicine, and the shock of it gentled him. 'Why am I so angry?'

'I don't know, boy. You've got another bar.'

'Oh, not that. Them. They are like so many hearty uncles with sour breath. Or a corral full of mules.'

'Mules, is it. Single file here. You go ahead.'

In an unpaved alley of sooty brick buildings Catto's mount stepped carefully between two ranks of coal-wagons. The afternoon remained cold, grey, barely tolerable. 'Something is wrong with me,' he went on when Phelan had caught up with him.

'You're bored.'

'More than that. For a moment there it was as if they were laying hands all over me.'

'You flatter yourself. My God, what a wind!'

'It is. Let's get out of it.'

'A few minutes more. I'm taking you to the hospital.'

'Oh are you? Why don't you tell me about all this?'

'Later. Ride in silence now, and think upon poverty, chastity and obedience.'

'I am a captain of infantry,' said Catto.

'And like all captains, you talk too much.'

Catto laughed aloud, and laughed a bit more, and said, or chanted, a ritual 'You son of a bitch', and felt better.

'He's a strange man,' Phelan repeated. 'Less so now because of that fiancée of his, that Miss Grosbeak or whatever it is.'

'Olivia Groesbeck. She's thirty-nine.'

'You dirty gossip.'

'Military intelligence,' Catto said primly.

'Thirty-nine is all right. Hooker's fifty. And her father owns half of Ohio including the railroads. That makes her young and beautiful.'

'The old fellow's a Democrat. I've heard him called a Copper-head. He hates Lincoln.'

'Well, so does Hooker. Anyway the point about Hooker is that his men come first, like sons. That's the only explanation I can give you. He wants them all to look up to him and worship him, and in return he takes care of them. When he had the Army of the Potomac he gave them furloughs and fresh veg-etables, and allowed Letterman to reorganize the whole medical service. You know medicine has always been a botch in the army. You've seen them swearing in cripples and consumptives, and leaving men to bleed to death.'

'I've seen you play at surgeon,' Catto said, and tossed down a drop.

'Yes, yes. Anyhow. Hooker cares. You remember when he said this country needed a dictator? He was angry because his men were dying with no need, and discipline did not exist any-where outside the books, and he blamed it on Lincoln, so he said that to some fool reporter.'

'What did old Abe do to him?' Catto thought of the President as possibly his uncle; at any rate a good Illinois man, not one of those New York fellows.

'Gave him the Army of the Potomac, put the future of the country in his hands, and wrote him that only successful gen-erals could appoint dictators.'

Catto rollicked. 'That's a man. That's a real man.'

'Oh, I suppose so,' Phelan said slowly. 'I am rather a Demo-crat myself.'

'A Democrat? A Democrat?'

'Now, now. There are a few, you know. But I like Lincoln well enough. Did you know the Eighth Wisconsin had a real eagle called Old Abe? They used to show him off. He would kill a rattler and they would bet on him.'

'I heard that.'

'So. About Hooker: he had Letterman set up divisional hos-pitals and put them together to make a corps hospital, and reform the ambulance service, and God knows how many men are running around today who should be dead. Thousands, thousands, and they owe it to Hooker. He is a nasty, unreliable

7

man, cold and full of self-conceit, but he stands up straight and he takes care of his men.'

Catto brooded. 'He spoke to me once about that. About pride. And taking care of your own, and so forth. I thought it was only bullshit.'

'It's more than that. Here, pour for yourself. So he is doing something like that here, putting together various services, and his boldest decision, daring and imaginative, was to place Surgeon Phelan in charge. Now I am a major and nobody will ever die again.'

'Oh that's sweet,' Catto said. 'That's good to hear. I wonder they didn't think of it earlier. How does that make me a captain?'

'Well, when he told me about this, and said I would be a major, I asked myself, what would give me the greatest pleasure? And the answer was, to give orders to Catto, and cuff him and kick him, and put official reprimands in his record. So I asked the general if I could bring in a company of the line to be my headquarters company, for guard duty and transportation and quartermastering, and he thought it was a good idea, and I overcame his objections to you by offering him half your wages. For reasons beyond me he thought you a wise choice. Also he laughed somewhat boisterously – I am not sure why. You'll bring both platoons into town and move them into the barracks on Broadway. Silliman is all the lieutenant you'll need so don't bother the general about another.'

'The big town at last.' A citified eternity yawned. 'And I thought I was rid of you.' The birds would soon be flying north, and the little furry fellows popping out of their holes, chipmunks and groundhogs and muskrats, and the dogwood flowering. He would miss that.

'Yes. And the work won't hurt you. You know, if you want to stay in and be a general you will someday have to learn to read and write and add simple figgers. Just for signing orders and reckoning your pay. A little administrative work will do you good. It's a clerk's world.'

They haggled for a moment, clerk-clark-clerk-clark.

'The war is really over now,' Catto said. 'You won't have any wounded. This is like a civilian hospital.'

'Well, yes. They'll all be in uniform, but survivors, not soldiers. We wanted to live through it and we did. Now we must set about improving the world.'

Catto was scandalized.

'Yes, yes,' Phelan said with a cock of the head and a minatory jab. 'Bind up the wounds. We've been doing the devil's work for years. Now we do God's work for a while. Listen, this is going to be some world. Believe me. We've all been killing each other for so long that the chance to do something else will bring the whole country to its knees in thanks. It's begun already. Convalescent camps. Who ever heard of such a thing?'

'They never sent me to one.'

'Ah, but you had Phelan in attendance. Anyway, some good will come out of this war. Much good. We're learning about gangrene and using needles more' – Catto shuddered – 'and not just pouring saleratus down every gullet. Even more.' He folded himself into meditation; his pits and wrinkles deepened, darkened. 'This war of brothers has made men sad, and taught them to stay their hand. You know Forrest and Morgan will not attack hospital trains. Some kind of madness is being worked away forever.'

'You believe that?'

'I see no other way,' Phelan said. 'We have reached the farthest insanity, brother killing brother or father son or son father. Either we go on through that and burst out the other side into some sort of righteousness, or the whole human race is doomed and Christ died for nothing.'

Catto grunted. 'You'll have me out of a job. You and Willich. He talks that way too. Well, we have nothing to do now but talk.'

Phelan smirked: 'There is always redskins to worry about. And we need fellows like you in trouble for further progress in the medical arts. What shall we do about pyemia? Septicemia? Amputations clean or flap? I favour the flap myself but we must learn to do better with abscesses. Doctor Moses Israel was very good with abscesses.'

'Doctor Moses Israel? You can do better than that.'

'He was with you and Rosecrans at Chickamauga and a famous good man.'

'A good man, was he?'

'Yes, he was, no worse than any other heathen. Don't be so bloody proud of your own piggish state. You are merely a Protestant with not much brow. I don't know which is worse, not to see the truth at all, or to see it and then turn away from it.' Phelan shook his head savagely and slapped a fat hand hard on the tabletop. 'This country! You love your little prides and your silly hates. The war is over, man! You've got to quit it now! I never saw such haters, not even in the old country where they know how. All day long I hear it. To hell with the Irish. To hell with the Germans. Everybody hates the French and the Italians, and God save the Poles and the Jews and the poor bloody niggers. All day long! You're all mad. North and South is the least of your troubles.'

'Well just look at the rolls and stop shouting at me,' Catto flared. 'The army is all Routledges and Franklins and Godwin-sons, Ross and Pierce and Morgan and Scott and Blake. All the old names. And where the hell are all those others you love so much? Home getting rich.'

'You're an ass,' Phelan said calmly. 'The whole country is ninety per cent old stock, so of course the army is too. You talk like we were still a colony and the king should keep those others out. Bloody Scottish bigot is what you are.'

'Bigot!' Catto half rose, fell back. 'Well, by Jesus. Maybe so. All right,' he said mildly, 'I'll think about that. And I'll allow as how Surgeon Moses Israel is a fine fellow. Just don't preach any more. Don't spoil this fine day. This fine week – the boy is well and walking, and at least nobody hates *him*.'

'That's true, that's true,' said Phelan with a cocky smile. 'So let us cheer up. And as I promised you, in fifty years the whole world will be Catholic anyway. Now let me show you my hospital, and you can wash up afterwards. I'll sell you my old bars.'

'By heaven, I just got a raise, too, didn't I.' For one bitter instant Catto wished that there were someone somewhere who might care about it, someone who might open a letter and say, 'Well, well. Marius is raised in pay.' There was always Charlotte. And Saturday night upon him. 'A raise,' he repeated. 'We must celebrate.'

Phelan grinned. 'It is all prepared. And no more wild rides through a cold countryside. We have a table for four at the Opera House Hotel, and two separate rooms.'

Catto stretched languidly, and moaned gentle mirth. 'Ah, Major. Ah, Major. Friend of my heart.'

'Roast pigeons, corn bread and beer,' Phelan promised.

'You have made me the happiest man in the world,' Catto said. 'Sell me those bars right now, and lend me a needle and thread.'

Monday morning Godwinson met him at the colour line and took hold of the bridle. Catto was pleasantly saddlesore, and dreamy, and self-satisfied, in the manner of lovers on Monday since the proclamation of Sunday. 'Godwinson,' he said lazily. 'Sergeant Godwinson. How goes it, man?'

'It's that fool Routledge,' Godwinson said, peevish.

'Never mind. We're about to make Routledge laugh out loud.' Catto swung out of the saddle.

But before his foot hit the ground Godwinson had said, 'No we aren't. He deserted Saturday. Went home. Left a note. Hey, you picked up the wrong coat somewhere.'

Chapter Six

One trouble with young Catto was an absence of history. 'Nothing. No family Bible, no papers. Just the name, and the one fact: he was a smith. A poor man, settled at a crossroads outside of town and bothered nobody. There was one old fellow who seemed to recollect, maybe, that they arrived sometime around eighteen thirty. So they were married for some time before I came along. Maybe there were others. Brothers. Sisters. Nobody knew. Here I am, then. Like a weed.'

'But a thinking weed,' Phelan said.

Catto frowned blankly. 'Don't know what that means. Point is I do wonder, I honest to God wonder. I used to make up histories. How we came over in sixteen twenty, or seventeen fifty, with some old Catto about seven feet high marching in front, and his good-looking wife right with him. And they settled down for a while and fought Indians and raised a crop and a family. I put them in Connecticut usually, what Jacob calls Connetic. Sometimes in Massachusetts, but I favoured Connecticut. They had some fierce battles in the early days.'

When the past failed he had the future, and lately his mind had embarked on some prodigious journeys. In moments of idleness or sleeplessness, many such now, and even when lying spent and dreamy beside, under, over or around his lady-love, he was persecuted by visitations, glimpses beyond the veil, episodes from the future life of His Worship General Lord Marius Catto, banal but exciting, like a series of boys' books: Marius Catto the Foxy Trapper (in the Oregon fur trade), Marius Catto the Lone Wolf (California Scout), Marius Catto the Corn God (Homesteader), the Leathery Cattle Baron, the Intrepid Indian Fighter, the prospector and his Mother Lode. He knew that all those lives had to be lived, all those deeds done, all those fights fought; he knew that it was young men like him who would live, do, fight, die, and he knew that he was the best of them and wondered often which life would be his. His mind tried to live those lives for him, to select the path most fitting, most right, most Catto.

In Cincinnati he saw Charlotte every weekend (a contempt, bred of familiarity, politely ignored, opening between them) and found himself living out an astonishing reversal, a perversion of nature: he made love to a live, warm, commercially enthusiastic woman almost at will, and in moments of private reverie he yielded to an upright, industrious, adventurous but womanless fantasy. He felt that he stood for the country as a whole; the United States of America – God's country, this field of honour, this land of plenty – had stood still for four years, achieving a crucial, inevitable, insane massacre, lancing a vast and bloody boil, and its people too had stood still, survived an agonized, frustrating travail; but soon this foolishness would be ended, and then God alone knew what the limits might be. Gold, land, game, fur, grain, meat, machines – room enough and goods enough and grass enough and sky enough for centuries to come; and soon they would all be free to jangle off and make their fortunes.

These journeys of the mind left him weary. They were indeed prodigious, and he returned from remote triumphs exhausted, buffeted, having encountered red-eyed beasts and carnivorous plants, eaten buffalo and snake, chaffered and haggled with Sioux, Mexicans, Russians. 'I have too much freedom,' he said to Silliman, 'so many things to do in life,' and that made him think of Jacob and reflect that Jacob might be the only man he knew to whom freedom was worth tears of joy, who would never in his life complain of too much freedom. Good enough, he thought. Maybe I did some good in this war. I have not lived in vain. By golly.

And where was Marius Catto, the saviour and prop of the beloved republic, when the War Between the States came to an end? Sad to tell he was standing buck naked at a third-floor window of the Opera House Hotel rubber-necking out at the

Fifth Street Market, the Burnet House, the river, where the big bridge would soon go up at the foot of Vine Street; standing there safe from the prying eyes of the vulgar, rubbing his belly in raccoon content, airing his woebegone adjutant, letting the blood resurge and blinking moronically at the metropolis that all unknowing harboured himself, this preposterous creature, half sphinx half chimera. He did not long pursue this sight-seeing. It was unnatural. Catto believed that tall buildings were about to fall down when he was in them, and often from a third-floor window he saw the earth – flower beds, cobblestones, packets of manure, pedestrians, wagons, stray cats, lamp-posts, barrels of rainwater and baskets of garbage – rush explosively to meet him; then he would grip the sill and close his eyes, or totter backwards to recover at full length on a rocking bed.

He turned away, but frowned in the act, his eyes travelling over the warm bed, the cradle of his joys and sorrows, and the dark sleeping woman, from here merely tumbled hair, a coarse cotton sheet. Shouts in the street drew him back, and he realized that he had been watching, half seeing, an agitated, flowing crowd; listening to, half hearing, a clamour not of the Lord's day. He leaned out; a breeze tickled his broad chest; the street was full. Men and women scurried, shouted, waved; coats flapped, dogs barked, wagons and gigs came to a standstill. A bottle smashed, a cry rose. Catto woke up and stared about. Three men boosted a barrel to the back of a wagon and pounded it open; liquid gushed – beer, he guessed – and insane revellers danced close, bearing mugs, steins, cups, a bucket; a boy took the stream full in his face, twitched and flopped, revolved grin-ning, flung up his arms, carolled a rebel yell. 'What the hell,' Catto said. 'Sunday?' He stood at the window fumbling with shirt buttons, confused, excitement rising.

He saw Thomas Martin. And Jacob. He was not surprised. The noontime air was heavy with portent. The two were stand-ing together, jabbering, in the doorway of a shuttered shop. 'Martin!' No use. 'Thomas!' No use. He loosed the buttons, doffed the shirt, waved it wildly.

He began to suspect, and choked out 'Good God!'

Slipping into the shirt again he turned to the bed. 'Charlotte!

Charlotte!' He rooted for his clothes, swept his shoes from beneath the bed. 'Charlotte!' A muffled babble. He slapped her behind. She groaned peevishly. He shook her; the faint odours of sleep rose. The room was close and abruptly alien. She rolled over and struggled up, blinking and drawn, the nightgown bunched at her waist. 'What are you doing?' she wailed sleepily, and he did not know this tired, squarish woman with gummy eyes.

'Look at me,' he said. 'Something's happened. You hear? I think maybe the war's over.'

She blinked more vigorously, gulped, and sat, eyes vacant, lower lip pendulous. 'The war?'

'The war,' he said. 'You remember. I've got to go back.'

'Nooo,' she whimpered. 'You come here. The war's over. Time to celebrate.'

He stared down upon her in vexation. 'No, my sweet friend. Not now. If it's true I've got to be with my men.' He buttoned his flies, buckled his belt. 'Damn that Routledge.'

'Your men!'

Catto laughed shortly, snorting like Godwinson. From the window, carnival: the world freed, sprung, its first exercise of liberty doubtless a monumental debauch. He jammed boots on to sockless feet, stuffed socks within his shirt, strode to his jacket, his hat, the plume bedraggled and dusty. 'Jesus. I can't believe it.' And he paused, because that was true: he could not believe it. There opened before him a bleak vista, icy, deserted: his future. He was a soldier, but being a soldier was already not the same thing.

'You wait a minute,' she said. 'You're not going to leave me here like this. What about Sunday dinner? And a cab?' As if the next payment were due, she covered her breasts haughtily, contriving to flaunt them also.

'For Christ's sake,' Catto said. 'I'll leave you money for dinner and a cab, but I've got to go.' He would keep Haller with him. Haller had good years left, and the stripes could be politicked somehow. He dug up a couple of dollars and set them on the chest of drawers. 'Here. Look, I'll see you next week. I'll send a note around.'

'Soldiers!' she snarled, and he stopped in alarm. 'You and your money. You and your men. Never mind next week.'

'Charlotte,' he pleaded half-heartedly, and reached to tousle her tousled hair. She ducked away, peeling off the sheet, and jumped to her feet, and he saw a squarish woman, running a bit to flesh, who could be dowdy in a nightgown. But he remembered more than that, and resolved to be gentle. 'This has been my life for four years. Since I was a boy this is all I know. I have to be with them now. That's how it is.'

After a moment she said sullenly. 'Oh, all right.' He thought how little he knew her.

'I'll send you a note,' he said.

'Don't trouble yourself.' She slouched to the basin, poured from the pitcher. Catto could think of nothing to say.

He closed the door with considerable relief.

And ran down the stairs and into the street, where he was whirled into a crazy reel, fiddler and all, with shouts and laughter breaking over him, and cries of 'Hey sojer!' A burly man in a round hat, a cloth knotted about his throat, squeezed the breath out of him and spilled whisky on his jacket, roaring, 'Good work, mate! You did it!' Catto freed himself and plunged into another mass of mankind. A shrill cur nipped at his boots. A woman kissed him: she had breakfasted on fish and beer. Catto laughed and slapped her rump and laughed again, standing on the cobblestones clutching his hat, thinking that it was not every day he slapped two rumps in ten minutes; he worked his way across the street slapping rumps, and counted seven before he flopped, panting and woozy, against the shutters of the small shop, a jeweller's, he saw. 'Thomas,' he blurted. 'Jacob. Is it true?'

'That's what they say. On the telegraph from Washington, they say. Lee surrendered this morning.'

'Lee.' Catto grinned foolishly.

The boy too smiled: Jacob nodded and nodded, quietly cheerful; and Catto nodded, and they stood for a time wordless.

'Thomas,' Catto said then, 'how are you? It's been a month now.'

'Just fine,' the boy said. 'A little tired. And what a scar! But the war is over.'

The carnival swirled before them, thundered and screeched, a fiddle here and a bugle there and a banjo somewhere else struggling valiantly against the press and holler, the bell and blare, the happy irony of rebel yells, the drunken whoops of victors who had never fought.

'How does it feel, Jacob?'

Jacob squinted up at the sun, amused: he rubbed the back of his neck. 'Feels good,' he conceded.

'Yes sir,' Catto said. 'It feels good. What will you do now?'

Thomas Martin too waited in friendly curiosity.

'Stay here,' Jacob said. 'Get some work. Maybe . . . maybe . . .'

'Maybe what?'

'Maybe find me a wife.' Jacob smiled, shy. 'I got – ' and he paused warily, looking from the captain to the boy, from the boy to the captain, visibly wrestling his way from the little privacy he owned towards an act of commemorative trust – 'I got almost a hundred dollars.'

Catto found himself moved by the confidence, and awkwardly sought a reply: 'Why, that's fine. That's more than I have right now.'

Gravely Jacob pursed his lips; gravely, sorrowfully, he nodded again; gravely he meditated; gravely he said, 'Lend you some, if you want.'

Startled, Catto stood blinking until Thomas Martin crowed laughter and Jacob smiled, and Catto understood, with immense shock, that he had once more been the butt of a joke. He chuckled appreciatively. The chuckle took hold suddenly, the joke seemed to be bursting, echoing, multiplying within him, and then he was whinnying, guffawing, rollicking in breathless and tearful jubilation, racked by a fierce, idiotic jollity, by gusts and bellows of joy and mockery, helplessly shouting cosmic peals of merriment, celebrating and deriding himself, Jacob, the boy, all men and women, all war and peace; the universe dissolved in this seizure of truth.

He recovered. He wiped his eyes on his sleeve and sobbed a

last laugh. 'I'm obliged to you,' he said. 'Maybe later. Right now I'm hungry. I'm off to the hospital. Thomas, what about you?'

'That's up to Gen'l Willich.'

'Yeh. But you get that rifle back and scoot out of here as soon as you can. Back to Greenup County. Hear?'

'Well, maybe,' the boy said.

Catto paused, feeling that more was required. 'Tell you what,' he said. 'You remind me some day, say ten years from now, and I'll buy you a dinner and tell you about the time I took a ball in the shoulder, back during the big war.'

'I never told you,' the boy said, 'but I was mad at myself for missing.'

They all grinned stupidly. On an impulse Catto shook the boy's hand, and then Jacob's.

Routledge, Routledge! That poor, sad, stupid old man! Soon or late they would find him, and he would pay. If only he had waited! Suppose the unlikely, that he had reached home: he would be skulking now, sleeping in the loft, diving for cover at a dog's yap. Lincoln had decreed an amnesty for deserters who rejoined their regiments by May tenth; Routledge might never hear of that, buried to his terrified eyes in hay, cowering at every alien footfall. Two days – if he had waited two days! Nine children. Catto imagined Routledge in prison, still a Jonah, stumbling over his own chains, turning an ankle on the ball, smashing his foot with the heavy sledge. Poor fool! So many of them were fools, Captain Catto not excepted. Franklin was a filthy fool. Padgett was an innocent fool. Silliman was a rich fool. Phelan was a wise fool. Hooker was the greatest fool of all because he had gone furthest among fools. Dunglas was a dangerous fool because he had stingy eyes and was elegant and graceful. Godwinson was a vain fool and Haller a bitter fool. Uniform of the day: cap and bells. All of them.

A rank of young girls shouted and blew kisses; he smiled politely and saluted, a loose wave. True, he had survived. That was not foolish.

Stunned, he halted: the war was over! He was alive and unhurt! All his limbs! With two bars and a fine moustache! Glory hallelujah!

Catto entered the hospital shouting for bread and coffee, and marched towards the day room. Godwinson and Carlsbach crossed him in the corridor and Godwinson's mouth flew open but Catto was saying, 'Right, right. I did it, as I promised. The men may present me with a gold watch.'

Carslbach thought that extremely clever and grew hysterical by degrees. Godwinson and Catto were slapping shoulders and muttering good things. 'Poor Routledge,' Catto said. 'Poor Routledge,' Godwinson said. 'Poor Routledge,' Carslbach said.

Catto went to his room, disinterred an exhausted toothbrush and smeared upon it a dab of ointment, a mysterious, vile-tasting and highly mutable substance invented by Phelan, constantly drying, flaking and diminishing in puffy, spontaneously generated clouds of white calx; the drawer was coated. He washed his face and stood there moist, adrip, scrubbing at his teeth, abrading away the night's frass, the yellow skin of war, the taste of the inner man. He spat, drank, buffed gently with a fresh tongue. 'Good morning all,' he said aloud, 'or whatever time it is,' and changed his clothes, not omitting clean socks. He donned slippers, extracted three cigars from a box and struck out for the day room, lightening the day further with cheery jibes for assorted cripples, amputees and simples, for one blind, one relatively jawless, one with a pack of dressings strapped to his middle like a money belt. In the day room he deflated himself, emptying his lungs in a growlish, relieved, relaxing gush. Home again. 'It is even he,' said Phelan.

'Marius!' Silliman beamed. 'You've heard.'

'Heard what?'

'The war. It's over, man. Lee surrendered.'

'Where's my coffee? What is this about a war?'

Silliman blushed perfectly.

Catto relented. 'Nice work, Ned. You scared them to death.'

Franklin entered, bearing a tray, and set it before his captain.

'Piggy,' Catto said.

'Yes sir?'

'The war is over.'

'I heard, sir.'

'You'll be going home soon.'

'Yes sir.'

'Where's that?'

'Decatur, sir.'

'Decatur. So I don't have to be nice to you any more.'

'No sir.' Franklin spoke warily, glancing from Phelan to Silliman, searching desperately for the point of the jest.

'Then I want to tell you,' Catto said lazily, 'and you will never know how much pleasure it affords me, that you are beyond all doubt and all comparison the filthiest, stinkingest soldier it has ever been my misfortune to serve with.' Phelan was smiling, but Silliman stared at Franklin with cold eyes. Franklin attempted a smile, gave it up, looked from one officer to another. 'I used to pray for rain,' Catto went on, 'because the stench of wet cotton was easier on the nostrils than the stench of dry Franklin. You're a dagtailed pig and you pollute the company and we are all sick of it. Now get out of here so I can eat.'

Franklin was white about the nose and mouth. 'Yes sir,' he managed, and faced about snappily and left them.

'Now why did you do that?' Phelan asked.

Catto bit into his bread and swigged coffee. 'That damned civilian! It did give me pleasure,' he said after a moment, and paused to swallow; 'ah, that's good, that's good. Thank God for coffee, even this coffee. It gave me pleasure, and I think it gave Ned pleasure, and it was a little revenge on behalf of the company, and ah! how I am sick of stinks, and it may have been the best thing anyone will ever do for Decatur. Also it was pleasant to act like an officer for a change and not a politician.' He showed his teeth; his eyes sparkled. 'By God, me lads. The war is over. I can get on out west now.'

'You can get on out west when Hooker says so,' Phelan grumbled.

'You're really going west, are you?' Silliman asked.

Catto smiled beatifically, warwhooped quietly, and stuffed his young self with bread and coffee.

110

All that week they traded news and gossip, and were uncomfortable with one another. Lee was finished but Johnston was still fighting, or was not; and Morgan; and Jessee; a small force of Johnnys still held out in Georgia; no, in South Carolina; no, in North Carolina; no, in Tennessee. Older men were sure to be sent home first. No, it was time in uniform that counted. No, it was how many battles. And how many wounds. No, the officers would make recommendations. 'I will recommend you all for garrison duty in the south,' said Catto, and was answered by gratifying jeers. 'None of you can be sent home until the last patient here is well.' More jeers. 'On the outside remember that if you are hungry or thirsty or need money, Silliman's father will be pleased to oblige.' Or, 'No claps released for two years.' Franklin did not chuckle, and Catto was now rather sorry to have bullied him. Farewell hung thick as fog, and the bad jokes were only feckless shafts of watery sunlight. 'It's a long time, three years,' he said to Silliman. 'If I was on the way out I'd be scared. I got habits now that don't mean much out of the army.'

'All the same,' Silliman said. 'I don't see how you can do it. They'll bust you down to sergeant probably, and on the outside you could go far. You could run a mill, handle men, maybe even go into politics. You've got that touch.'

'Politics!' Catto did his best to look ashen. 'Christ Almighty, Ned. Mind your language.'

'You know what I mean,' Silliman rebuked him. 'You're a leader. But a wiseacre too.'

'Piss-ant lieutenant. Watch what you say, lad. I'll have you burying horses.'

'No, I mean it.' Silliman coloured again, suffused by his own solemnity. 'You listen to me for a minute, Marius. You're a fine man, but you've got to learn to take things seriously. You could rise straight to the top of the heap.'

'And sit at Hooker's right hand.'

'I mean outside.'

'I don't know one damn thing about outside. I know everything about inside.'

'You're better than the army.'

'That'll do. The army's been mother and father to me. Anyway I want to try the cavalry now. I'm tired of mud and I'm

111

tired of walking and I like the smell of horses. Also their conversation.'

'Go to the devil,' said Silliman.

Men washed. Some shaved. Some sorted out the petty acqui-
sitions of the war and turned up, or discarded, strange objects.
Franklin owned a crucifix that made him uneasy; he showed it
off, blustering – heavy silver, finely wrought, nails, gash, crown
of thorns – but he wriggled and frowned, hazily glimpsing his
own blasphemy: robbing the dead of Christ himself! Jesus!
Lowndes had a snuff-box, Carlsbach a small pistol four inches
long, a muzzle-loader with the ramrod cunningly lodged along
the barrel. Catto would not have tolerated wedding rings. A
collector of dead men's wedding rings had no place in his company. He suspected that some of his boys had gleaned jewelled
rings on one or another battlefield. That was all right; it was
not the value of the piece that mattered. Even in God's country
a man had to get ahead the best way he could. But a wedding
ring.

He himself had tried to live a lean life, free of the claims and
bonds of possessions, but he had lately become a fearful mag-
pie, what with half a dozen bright kerchiefs to wear with an
open shirt when the weather turned hot, and a box of cigars,
and extra underwear, fine linen, and a small leather box con-
taining written statements of commission, a jeweller's receipt, a
photograph of Charlotte and himself, a memorandum of names
and addresses. He also had a housewife, scissors, needles and
thread, comb and brush, all rolled in a square of white canvas,
and a writing set, a tablet of paper and a pen with several nibs,
and a bit of dry ink and some envelopes. With his issue of uniforms and arms and bedding, his mess kit, his manual of tactics,
his soap and razors and toothbrush and paste, with Phelan's
little book on medical supplies, and some spare insignia and a
spare tassel for the hilt of his sword – good God! He stared
about his cubicle in amazed distaste. Time to move on!

But while waiting upon the pleasure of history and politicians,
glowering and mooning, sacked by circumstance, he was flung

for comfort to professionals like Colonel Bardsley, and disturbed to find so few. 'Hell no,' the colonel said on the Tuesday. 'There won't be ten of us left, and none whatsoever of the rank of private soldier.' He and Catto sat alone in the visitors' saloon of the hospital and puffed wearily at cheroots. 'You're beginning to feel it now, hey? I feel it too.' Colonel Bardsley was a widower. 'We'd be better off in the field, in a camp somewhere. It isn't only the sense of being left alone, all those civilians swarming home and leaving you in sole and permanent possession of all the army's goods and chattels including cannon, horses, *pediculi vestimenti,* New Testaments and useless chaplains. That's an odd feeling right there, like being left a general store or two, but that's not all of it. The worst is Cincinnati. Or New York or Chicago, any city, because there you are among the heathen, the money-changers like that fellow Groesbeck or those shipping people who've already raised their riverboat fares in high expectation of a fancy business the next few months, and you look at Cincinnati, and listen to it, and smell it, and it comes over you that there never *was* a war, that a great fraud has been perpetuated. I think this has been happening since long before Jesus Christ.'

The colonel was pale of face now, a stark edge of brightness to his blue eyes, his skin taut as if he would soon sweat, and he seemed less a colonel, much less the feed-and-grain magnate that Catto had at first fancied him, and more a peasant too long from home. 'They have been taking men by the crotch and lining them up and forging chains on to them since the memory of man runneth not to the contrary. They have been marching them up and down the field of honour and sticking swords and arrows into them and blowing holes through them. And the men breathe hard and smile foolish smiles and sometimes laugh – like when it is the next fellow has his balls blown off or his belly blown open. Then they close ranks and march on, and the enemy kills them from in front and their officers – not to say their mothers and the politicians and whatever other speechmakers can glorify themselves by instigating young men to rush off and commit suicide – kill them from behind, and they smile their foolish smiles and spin about once and drop dead. For

8

good. And then the war ends, like right now, and the survivors, all your men there, they're all saying "You see? I came through! I came through!" and they'll come and have a drink with the officer who was telling them yesterday to charge. They were fools before this week but now they are bigger fools because they think it is over and they won and right has triumphed and virtue reigns and all such.' The colonel was crying. He was leaning forward in his chair with his forearms on his knees and his hands drooping, and the cigar smoke spiralled straight up into his pouched eyes, and he was crying, shedding tears steadily and swallowing sobs. 'I lost two sons, Catto. I lost two sons. I don't care that it's over. You understand that? I wouldn't care if it went on forever.'

And the poor man had to make a speech on the Wednesday. Catto listened to it in burgeoning pain. Moment of victory. Great joy to all soldiers. George Washington. Many of you soon home. Bind up wounds. Swords ploughshares. However. Paper work. Still fighting. Soon. Soon. Congratulations. Thank you men.

And then some damn fool called for three cheers for the colonel. Catto fled. In the corridor a dead patient was being trundled to his last-but-one resting place. Bad week to die. Senseless. Catto went to the visitors' saloon and sat in the gathering dusk. On or about the eleventh day of May he would re-enlist. Perhaps he would feel better then. He might do it sooner. He felt bad now, enduring the sweats and incipient nausea. That evening there was comic relief: the announcement of a victory celebration. 'Ah, you see,' said the colonel. Friday Night 14 April 14 Public Landing. City of Cincinnati. Martial Music, Pyrotechnical Wonders. Our Heroic Boys. Catto sulked heroically and boyishly, and dispatched an invitation to Charlotte, fat frowzy companion of his revels, big-bubbed bargain, thief of his youth, innocence and small gold.

Ah, but she would not reply. 'She noticed your cloven hoofs,' Phelan said, 'and is terrified.' Catto answered appropriately but in distraction, saddened. Phelan and Nell were still friends, so on Friday Night 14 April 14 Catto found himself approaching

114

the Public Landing at the corner of Broadway and Front with a fresh cockade on his campaign hat, a burning thirst in his throat, and gallant Neddy Silliman on his arm. 'I will not spend the evening with you. I am not accustomed to companions of your station in society.'

'My mother's father was Portuguese,' Silliman said.

'A *Portagee*?'

'Yes sir.'

'For God's sake. All this time. If I'd known you were a dago.'

'Besides,' Silliman said, 'your own family may have been clan chiefs. You may be related to somebody like James One.'

'James One,' Catto mused. 'Marius Catto, heir to thrones.'

The two stood among a gathering press, Catto uneasy, foolish as always among a crowd of civilians, Silliman calm and curious, contriving with no effort to make it plain that this festival was in his honour. In a special area for high dignitaries milled small men with round heads, and their wives in complicated hats. It was the number of children that disquieted and ultimately daunted Captain Catto. Whines arose, snarls, snuffles, sobs; here the orphan boy retained absolute pitch, and he foresaw an evening of misery, leavened only by petty thievery, an unplanned and possibly fatal explosion, half a drowning.

Silliman cocked a knowing eye. 'You're unhappy.'

'I could commit murder,' Catto said, 'I am that unhappy. This is madness, Ned. A Sunday school. Mark my words. There will be hymns sung. Some of these little bastards are wearing white shoes.'

'This is America,' Silliman protested gently. 'All the good people.'

'All the good people,' Catto murmured. In the torchlight, furling and leaping, he saw few faces: only mouths, caps. In the enclosure silk hats and mild bustle. Dogs yelped. A faint odour of fish, of bilge. How strong, he wondered, was the public landing? Hundreds might die in Cincinnati this night, like a thank-offering to the insatiable gods of war. He stepped aside, was thanked by a pretty face, and swept his hat low, making a leg in the small space allowed him. As he straightened, a preparatory rocket fired the night, from the landing or from a barge he could not tell. The rocket burst red. 'I think my moment has come, Lieutenant.'

'Now, now. The fun has just begun. Look at that!' A rocket blossomed white and Silliman stared up, eyes full of delight, mouth full of fine teeth.

'No, Ned. You stay. I'll see you in the morning.' Somewhere a band struck up. Catto groaned and slipped away. In a moment he looked back, and saw hundreds gaping like baby birds at the blue glow, and wondered why he had come at all. Two trulls carolled in chorus, and he ached for California.

But settled for less, touching his hat politely and walking briskly westward on Water Street, which resembled a good many Water Streets. Stragglers panted to him and past. 'It's the other way, Captain.' Catto saluted, waved, smiled aimlessly, dodged a rattling trap. In a patch of black he paused and listened to distant cries, to river birds, to the twist and creak of his own leather, to his own breast, his own inner beast, his own sad sigh. He stood still. This was better, he thought. Alone and invisible. I imagine it will be much like this from now on. Several decades of honourable service, a pension then, a good deal alone and the less visible the better.

There it is. The life of Marius Catto. Messages from on high tonight. Catto: you will not be a trapper. Catto: you will not be an explorer. Catto: you will not be a homesteader. Catto: you are a killer by trade and a fornicator by inclination, and that is all you are.

And after a moment: better than being a fornicator by trade and a killer by inclination.

He laughed, and wondered if he could remember that for Phelan. Then he moved along, out into the dim and shifting lights, making his way west with no plan or purpose, but a grand, triumphal drunk. What else? Perhaps a bit later he would make a speech. After all, this night should be marked.

It was marked chiefly by its end, though bits and pieces of it remained memorable. The door he pushed open admitted him to a scene of great evil, namely villainous drinkers of Irish

116

aspect and, like a portent, the most deformed, hostile, ravelled cat he had ever seen. He was a step inside before he knew he should not stay, but by then he was a captain of infantry in a position to demonstrate courage and insouciance, so there was no turning back. His mind had already linked a chain – Irish-Democrat-Copperhead-Kentucky-Confederate – and even in that brief moment the lamplight seemed to dim, the heat to rise, as if each of these momentarily motionless men would show him a face of one eye, the other horribly gouged, and a scar from lip to ear, and no teeth whatsoever. All he could do was walk the five steps to the wooden bar, nod to the barkeep and say, 'Whisky. You haven't seen a major called Phelan?'

'Phelan?' The barkeep, while stocky and low of brow, had pleasant brown eyes and no scars beyond the nick of a razor on his right cheek. 'Phelan? Any of you fellows know an officer name of Phelan?'

'He's a surgeon,' Catto plunged on, 'at the hospital, and he likes a drink from time to time. Told me he knew of a nice place not far from the gas works.'

The barkeep served him. 'There's about a thousand places not far from the gas works. But Phelan is a good name. Have a drink.'

Laughter. Catto raised his glass to the half-dozen, all old men, and drank. The tavern might once have been a stable; it gave off that implacably wooden air, odour: heavy, bare, shredding posts and ancient, rough pine planks. Four or five tables and the bar, huge jugs of water and no taps. And the old-timers, bowed, grizzled, hairy. We are now in the year nineteen hundred, Catto thought, and you are looking at six Cattos. Calm now but curious, he made an effort to shrink. Your buttocks are withering and stringy. Your belly bellies. You have pale flat paps. You have not shaved for a week and your eyes lie deep in powdery leather pouches. Between your legs hangs another, smaller, pap, surmounted by a noodle. Breathing is a work of serious proportions, and every morning is a surprise.

He drank again. Nonsense. You are the flower of the age. 'The war is over,' he said.

The barkeep nodded. 'It is that. And a good thing. Though when I was your age I liked a bit of a fight. And what will you

do now?' In the half-light of two lamps the brown eyes wel-
comed Catto.

'Get drunk.'

'That too I liked.'

'Then join me. One for everybody.'

A murmur answered, and a shuffle; two of the old men
joined him at the bar, and one gestured back to a third with
an old man's slow urgency. The third grinned and rose, nodding
towards them. What a place to die, Catto mused. The air was
warm. He set his hat on the bar and smoothed his moustache.

'My name is John,' the barkeep said, 'and this is old Robert
and Brendan, and the gaffer next to you is only Fitz. They drink
beer but I'll join you in a bit of the real.'

'What about those others?'

'They don't drink,' John said. 'Not after a certain hour. They
are now saturated and will sit there like kegs until thrown out.'

Catto laughed and said, 'This is a fine place.'

'I wish more thought so. Well, welcome to you, Captain . . . '

'Trout. Isaac M. Trout. Your health.'

'And yours, Captain Trout. I hope you drink like one:'

'I will tonight. Let's just set a bottle here and see what be-
comes of it.'

'The only way,' said stocky black-haired John. Catto thought
of stocky black-haired Charlotte and dismissed her with annoyance. John went on: 'Did you have a bad war?'

'Show me a good war,' Catto said. 'Either people are shooting
at you or you are sitting about staring at a wall.' He remembered
his manners and dug for a dollar. John remembered his own
manners and ignored it. 'But I suppose it's enough to have lived
through it.'

In an hour he was heartily bored but had drunk enough to
be telling them about Stones River. Old Fitz nodded, beady-
eyed, and soon the others drifted away, and a customer came
in, astonishing Catto, who had begun to understand that this
place, this scene, had a certain permanence to it, that at any
hour of the day or night it would comprise John and the same
five ancients, and that his own intrusion might be remembered
eternally, sung from father to son. Och. It was the night of the

great celebration, it was, and this buckeen Trout marches in, he does, all shined up with a feather in his hat, and he says, Drink up all. And then he goes on and on about a place called Stones River where he caught a ball in the behind. Now I ask you, how does a man catch a ball in the behind? Running away, that's how. But he was free with his silver.

Wet-eyed Fitz nodded, smiled, blinked and bleared, buried his veined nose in froth.

Catto broke open, and spewed autobiography. It was the absence of a clock. Time could be measured, or guessed, only by words or the level of the whisky. With the second bottle, John and a number of strangers assisting, he veered to Charlotte, and old Fitz nodded solemnly. 'What does it mean?' Catto asked him. Fitz shook his grey head. 'I'm fine without her. Don't know much about the lady so I have nothing to think about except . . . well, you know, and when you think about that she might be anybody at all. You understand. Cash on the pillow.'

Fitz was a great one for nodding. Some hours and many stories later in the evening, or morning, Catto bowed out for a moment to empty himself against a wall, remembering in some confusion the dire punishments visited, hip and thigh, root and branch, on every man that pisseth against a wall, and in the drunken black silence he understood for the first time that these were not punishments for illegal pissing but compassion for blameless tots. Phelan of course knew that. Damn Phelan.

He found Fitz unchanged, swaying gently, quenchless, yea a hogshead. 'I look forward to the west,' Catto said. 'We will civilize the place, but not too quickly. Plenty of room for fellows like me. John! Another one for the house. Trout is here!' He offered that in dim, instinctive wisdom, something must be done about this bottle and he could not do it alone. Not long after, or perhaps long after, there were hands at his armpits and knees, and he was muttering thanks, assuring John that he would be on his way shortly, fearing, but with no real passion, for his money, his boots – 'My hat! My hat!' – 'It's all right, Captain. We've got your hat right here.' – 'The war's over, you know.' – 'Yes sir, Captain. The war is over. You just take it

119

easy now for a while.' – and his belt – 'Fitz knows all about me. Anything you want to know,' the lamps bobbing and spinning, 'whoooo! you just ask whoooo! old Fitz. I told him whoooo! about my father too. Not really a smith, you know. He followed the horses. You won't say anything. Whoooo! Jesus! With a wagon and a bucket. Municipal employee, you under – whoooo!' – 'Don't you worry a bit, sir. Old Fitz is a fine man. Stone deaf but a fine old man.'

The sun woke him, and a murmur. He forced his eyes open. He saw a boy of ten or so, in patched britches and a filthy shirt. The boy's nose was a cornucopia of tadpoles and snails, and Catto shut his eyes tight; when he opened them again he saw a calm ring of interested citizens. He was in the street, lying against a brick wall, his hat sitting modestly upon his crotch, his buckle twinkling up at him.

He sat up. 'Take that boy away,' he croaked. He clapped the hat to his pumpkin head and sat breathing heavily, his tongue half out. He lowed hoarsely and licked his lips. Pride of the Union. He drew up his knees, and the action released a vile belch. 'The name,' he said, 'is Isaac M. Trout.'

'Well you better get up, Captain Trout,' a man said. He was fat and bearded, and wore a wool hat like a sailor. 'They killed Mister Lincoln last night.'

Chapter Seven

'I used to do all the right things on the Fourth of July,' Catto mourned. 'Choke up, and hate the English; one year I went three months without telling a lie or swearing. All the churches cooked up beans or meatballs, and the band wore three-cornered hats. One time Stephen Douglas stopped by and made a speech. A lot of us went fishing or thieving but I always stayed to hear the band, and the volley. I saw my first soldier at one of those, a captain with a blond beard, a courtly man, bowing, saluting. I would have sold my soul to be him.'

'And now you are.'

'And now I am, and fought a war, and what the hell for. No, I don't mean that. What for wasn't so important. It was a great country and if a war had to be fought it was not for me to ask questions. I believed. How could you not believe in Mister Lincoln? And when the war is over we will all join hands again – that was a promise. If I had to go around shooting people, at least I knew that there would be an end to it, and we could get on with more important things. Not that I've put much stock lately in all the pretty sentiment. That's for the children. All I wanted was to snake my way through, and in the end I would be something – a soldier or a scout or a trapper, or at the worst a grocer or a cigar wholesaler or a bank clerk. Make a living, get children, live to be an old man.'

'Move your chair,' Phelan said, 'and stop squinting into the sun.'

Catto hitched his chair around, clattering and scraping. He sat like a schoolboy with his hands flat on his thighs, his head bowed, his full lips pursed in a fat pout, his eyes dull and sad. 'I was thinking of one of my masterpieces. It was a running shot, at an angle, and he spread his arms and went down on his face and slid along the grass that way. I was proud of it.'

'And now you're not.'

Catto shook his head slowly.

'All this because of Lincoln.'

'Well, maybe I'm growing up. But I cried, Jack. I cried. That's for Europe, killing kings. Not for us. I'd like to move out of here and maybe settle in a whole new country some-where. Or make one. On an island.'

'Go back to Scotland.' Phelan smiled half-heartedly. He rolled the r's richly: 'Surround yourself with freckled get.'

'It was all over. Lee kept his sword. And now Lincoln is in a box on that train and the country is worse off than it was five years ago.'

'No. Five years ago there was a war coming. That much at least is done. Otherwise I can't cheer you up. I can only recom-mend that you start drinking again and remember that every-body dies.'

'Right. All men are created equal as soon as they die.'

'*Omnia –* '

'I know. Well. I suppose I better get over this. I wonder if that fellow Booth was proud of himself.'

'Go to Charlotte.'

'For Christ's sake, Jack. I can't even spell her last name.'

'Go to Charlotte. The flesh is half the cure for grief.'

'And half the cause of it. She doesn't like me any more. I wonder if Hooker's happy. He hated the man.'

'Hard to say about Hooker. He's off in Springfield now, for the funeral.'

'Oh, they'll all be there. With their heads bowed, mumbling all the right things. And thinking how he should have promoted them faster.' Catto rose. 'I'm going out to walk around. A nice sunny day. I must see if the people are still grateful to their heroes.'

'They're still in mourning. This has been a quiet city, with the Copperheads afraid to say a word out loud.'

'Mm. Tell me something, Jack.'

'Your servant.'

'What's all this about the Catholics? Some rumour. Anything in it?'

'Why do you ask me?' Phelan glared. 'Do I look like an assassin? They need somebody to blame, you know. If something goes wrong and there's one Catholic in it, it's a plot straight from the Pope.'

'Cheer up,' Catto said. 'In fifty years we'll all be Catholic. I have it on good authority.'

'May your spleen wither, boyo.'

Catto fled the surgeon's curse.

He stood at the river with Silliman and they pitched pebbles into the scummy backwash. Silliman had aged, and appeared at least twenty-one. 'You'll be off soon,' Catto said.

'A couple of weeks. I suppose my father saw to that.'

'Don't apologize. Country needs folks like you.' A momentary rage gripped Catto: 'Don't let those stay-at-home rangers run things. You get in there and go to Congress or some such thing.'

'Maybe I will.' Silliman skimmed a flat stone at a placid river bird: the white bird squawked once and beat upward. 'Come with me. You work the mill while I make laws to favour you.'

'You're a generous fellow and I thank you. I suppose everything's possible for you. Lucky man. Some bright young thing waiting too.'

'Several,' said Silliman, and blushed.

'Damn liar. I bet you never yet had your hand – '

'Never mind now. What about it? You have nowhere to go. Might as well make money.'

'I've thought of it. Let's get out of here.' They turned away, and trod cobblestones towards the centre of the city. Catto was calmer of mind in the noonday sun; even in Cincinnati spring smelled good, the air a heady compound principally of manure and beer, yet fragrant. 'I can't decide now. Been feeling too low lately.'

'Me too. But you've only got a week or so.'

'Six days. But I could always let the hitch run out, and sign on later.'

'As a private.'

'Yeh. I had some higher rank in mind.' Catto was sleepy. The sun warmed his back and he remembered that day in the meadow, Thomas Martin rising like an angel to shoot him dead. Not a hundred miles from here. 'Trouble is, old Ned, I don't want to sign on for something and find out later I'm wrong for it. Hell of a thing if you put me in the mill and I turned out to be a born poet.'

'But there isn't time to try everything.'

'True. I always thought that when the war was over I'd know. Have a vision. Instructions: Catto, rise up and go breed hogs. Instead of which they kill my president.'

'Mine too.'

'I thought once I might travel. Go to work on a boat. See the old country.'

'You won't see much without money. They pay about a dollar a week on boats. And you eat garbage.'

'Well, that's out.'

They walked on, inspecting shops.

'It's all so strange,' Silliman said. 'Everything so empty. Like the sun would never set again. A war is your whole life, and when it ends you just stand there blinking.'

'That's how it is, all right. And I been in longer than you. Where we walking to, anyway?'

'Oh, anywhere,' Silliman said. 'Let's go up and smell the canal. This is one city I don't plan to return to, and I might as well experience it to the full.'

Catto smiled. 'Now look at that. You made me cheer up.'

'Good God,' said Silliman. 'Next thing you'll be drinking again.'

They laughed, puzzled and ashamed, and fell silent once more, edging away from wagons and loaders and stacked baskets as they crossed a market square.

'How long do you suppose people feel this way?'

'I don't know. Never had a war end before. Or an assassination.'

'No.' Silliman was grave. 'When the news came, or when I made myself believe it, I remember thinking I ought to keep close track of how I felt and what people said and all that, so I could tell my children about it someday. But all I remember is this gloomy, grey sort of sadness.'

Catto nodded and began an answer, but jumped a foot when the welkin dissolved in a sudden shimmering, golden clangour. The two stared upward. Bong. 'Saint Peter in Chains,' Silliman said. 'Look at that.' Bong. 'Over two hundred feet tall.'

'That's some bell.' Bong. 'Must be noontime. It rings slow.'

'It's for the funeral,' Silliman said.

Bong, sang the great bell, and Catto thought, bong. Bong. He drew in a deep breath, trying to open his throat, but it contracted and tears sprang to his eyes; he fought them down, swallowed, took another breath, and could not look at Silliman. The bell boomed on, and Catto stood with his head down and his hat brim hiding his hot eyes, and said good-bye to Mister Lincoln. Good-bye, Abe. Good-bye, Mister President. Good-bye, good-bye, good-bye.

He dreamed that night, dreamed a story the men told, of the girl who cropped her hair and enlisted to be with her brother. It was said to have happened in Massachusetts, in New York, Ohio, Illinois and Wisconsin, in 1861, 1862, 1863 and 1864, and the girl was fifteen, sixteen, seventeen, eighteen, nineteen, never older; had black, brown, red or blonde hair; but invariably this sort of bosom – I mean to say, how could she possibly have bound it down, and what a loss to mankind! In his dream they found her in a grove with the horse sergeant, and Catto watched writhing and fuming. It was Hooker who caught them, and no escape; Catto leapt to his feet and covered his nakedness with one hand while saluting with the other, but it was insufficient, no hand could cover this unruly upstart, this extravagant indecorum. As a flag passed by in his dream, and a drummer-boy, Catto awoke; behind the drummer-boy a caisson clattered and rumbled under the weight of a coffin. He was sick with loss, and lay still hoping to recapture sleep, the woman, the consoling warmth; but hoping was a daylight activity, and woke him further.

Later he remembered the dream and pondered it, because he had little to do, whiling away a Friday morning like the ten-toed sloth he was, scribbling orders for batting and socks and fresh pork; he understood that he had dreamed about his sorrow, about Lincoln, perhaps about the sweet young lady he had yet to meet. But the horse sergeant? His own base behaviour? He goggled at the memory of it, and was still smiling when the door flew open. He looked up in query, which altered to amiable welcome when he saw Jacob, but when Jacob said, 'They goin' to kill Thomas,' Catto betrayed unmannerly disgust, despairing of this black man who got things wrong, who could misunderstand what had doubtless been a perfectly plain, if unfunny, joke; already another thought was forming, a knowledge not yet knowledge because not yet made word, given flesh, image, but there, lurking and looming; so Catto sat back fighting irritation and fear, laughter and terror – as if his spirit were crying out, 'I will not hear this' – and said to Jacob, 'Don't be a blockhead.'

'Gen'l Willich say they have to kill Thomas.' Jacob's eyes shimmered.

Catto set down his pen in utter stupidity. 'It was like I was suddenly turned into a potato,' he said to Phelan next day. 'I know I quit breathing, and I think my blood quit running. After a moment I remembered that this country was a madhouse and Jacob might even be right. I got up in a hurry then and knocked some papers off the table and went out in the street and ran. I just left Jacob standing there. I also left my hat, so I was out of uniform the whole rest of the day. My blouse was open and the damn belt flapping. People looked at me and shied off, like the war might be starting up again and this crazy captain was rushing to save the city. I hooked up the belt while I ran. God knows what I looked like when I got to McLean Barracks.'

Today there was a sentry but Catto was a whirlwind. 'Stand aside,' he called, and took the steps in one leap. He plunged through the doorway, glided a long three steps to Willich's door and burst into the general's office. He saw several figures and perceived that he was among gentlemen of the first importance, so shook his head quickly, panting, and looked Willich in the eye and said, 'What is all this?' Then he groped for buttons and again became a soldier, huffing, blowing, doing up his blouse and standing rather straight.

126

Willich said 'Captain Catto' like a man still asleep. Catto knew then that it was all true. He recognized the others: Dickson, that was, and Stallo, and in a corner Captain Booth, who was Willich's adjutant. He remembered the morning sky, cottony clouds.

Dickson asked, 'Who are you?'

'Captain Catto, Judge. What is this about the boy?'

'What does it matter to you?' Dickson was annoyed.

Catto stared coldly.

'We are all here to do what we can,' Judge Stallo said, and Catto nodded without hostility, recalling that this man was a physicist, mathematician, philosopher and so on, and also the number one Deutscher in the city. *Alle menschen.*

He turned back to Willich. 'Please. Tell me what's happened.'

'Yes. Sit down,' said the general. 'What's the time?'

'Close to nine, sir,' Booth said.

'Where is Hooker anyway?' Catto asked.

'En route. We're trying to find him. A message. We cannot do this.'

'Do what? Will you please tell me, sir.'

'President Johnson has signed the order for Thomas Martin's execution,' Stallo declared formally.

Catto restrained a bellow. 'Do you mean Lincoln never tore it up? You mean you just left it on a desk in Washington all this time?'

'At that level there is nothing we can do,' Stallo said.

'It was Hooker,' Dickson said angrily, almost shouting, accepting Catto. 'Damn the man! He was *cleaning out his files*, if you can believe it, and he found the signed verdict. He'd forgotten all about it. He inquired whether sentence had been executed.'

'And it had not,' Willich said.'We had never received an order to execute the boy. Lincoln would not sign it; he would not pardon the boy but he would not sign the order. He hated to sign them. So I told Hooker about the boy. I was laughing. I was laughing! That day he wired for authority to carry out the sentence, and the President signed an order. Hooker ordered me to shoot the boy and went off to Springfield. I said nothing until last night because I could not believe that there would be no intervention, from Washington, from Hooker himself.'

'A frightful man,' Stallo said.

'It seems there was no one to plead for a pardon,' Willich said softly. 'If only his mother had been alive to plead for a pardon. Lincoln was free with pardons.'

'Where is the boy's rifle,' Catto asked tonelessly. 'This is madness.'

'Locked up,' Booth said. 'What about it?'

Catto and Booth exchanged the easy direct nod of comrades, professionals, men of an age; like regretful farmers on a pitching steamer they nodded. 'Where's the boy?'

'Also locked up.'

'Well let's get him out of here,' Catto said, 'and across the river.'

'Captain!' That was Willich. But silent Booth understood.

'You are in the presence of two judges and a general,' Stallo said sharply.

'Who I take it – with all respect, sir,' Catto said as drily as possible, ' – would rather see a boy murdered than risk General Hooker's displeasure.'

'No one has been murdered,' Dickson said, 'and it is not a matter of General Hooker's displeasure, I assure you. You will permit me to point out,' and Dickson was also dry, 'that we have just fought a war to preserve government by law and not by impulse. Please, Captain. We are here to find a way out, and not to outrage your finer sensibilities.'

'Take a cigar, Captain,' said Willich, and wood whispered upon wood.

'Yes, thank you, thank you,' Catto said rapidly. 'And when is this lunatic order to be carried out?'

'At noon today,' Willich muttered; Catto bent almost double like a man with the cramp, and just before he raised his angry face he brought a bitter iron captain's fist marteling down upon Willich's desk, hurting himself and striking up a mad dance of nibs. 'Booth. Can you and I get him out and away?'

'No,' said Booth.

Catto was instantly calm. He gazed at the three older men with a helpless, earnest curiosity.

Dickson spoke first: 'Captain Catto, Captain Catto, we all feel as you do.'

'Then let's do something,' Catto said.

'We are telegraphing to all likely stops on Hooker's route,' Stallo said. 'A slim chance, but a chance. Then, Judge Dickson has asked Mister Gaither to send a telegram directly to Major Eckert, who will take it personally to Secretary Stanton.'

'Who is Gaither?'

'Superintendent of the Adams Express Company,' Dickson said. 'My dear Captain, who are you and why are you suddenly in command?'

'My apologies,' Catto said wearily. 'I am merely a captain of infantry, in charge of the hospital company, and I am the fellow who brought the boy in, long ago, and was shot by him, and I am the only man in the world who has any cause to dislike him. But I like him. I don't know him very well, but I like him. Nobody knows him very well, but that doesn't matter. *I'll* plead for the pardon. I'm not the boy's mother, but I'm his *victim*. By God, General Willich!' He rounded abruptly, ferociously. 'The boy has been your, your, your *page boy* for half a year. How can you? How can you?' Willich was still. 'And who is Eckert?'

'Superintendent of the military telegraph,' Stallo told him. 'Major Thomas Eckert. He may be influential, and he will certainly be quick. On election night last year President Lincoln sat up with him, in the telegraph room, receiving the returns.'

'God bless Major Eckert,' Catto said. 'And I take it none of you gentlemen will mind if I keep vigil with you. No, of course you won't mind. Oh, what insanity!' He flopped into a soft leather chair, lit his cigar, and dropped the match into a copper ashtray strapped to the chair's arm. 'A black man brought me the news. The boy's friend. Free now, you understand. All men are created equal.'

Willich raised his shaggy grey-blond head. 'Captain Catto.' His voice was once more the voice of a general. 'That will be all. I want you to stay, but I want you to remember your place. And remember too that we may bear this day to our graves.'

'Then – '

9

'No. Nothing you can say has not been said already this morning.'

'I'm sorry,' Catto murmured. 'Can nothing else be done? Can I see the boy?'

'You may not see the boy,' Willich said. 'He is locked up in this building, and you may not see him. Father Garesche is with him. And you should know that I have ordered a firing squad to be made ready, and the place will be the big ravine on the Walnut Hills road, above the Deer Creek Valley and below the Pendleton house.'

Catto closed his eyes.

'You must understand, Catto,' Stallo said. 'This is a terrible period. Washington is full of grief, confusion, even hysteria. Against the rebels, against unnamed conspiracies. Seward wounded, Lincoln dead, how are they to know who is the next target?' Grave, ambassadorial, he turned to Willich. 'Do you know,' he said pensively, 'there is something else that could be done. A telegram to Johnson himself. Signed by the three of us, and Pendleton, and perhaps a few other first citizens.'

'Who's Pendleton?' Catto asked.

'Who's Pendleton?' Stallo was astounded, reproving. 'The Democratic candidate for vice-president last year. That is who. And Judge Dickson's wife is a cousin of Mary Todd Lincoln. That might help.'

Dickson said, 'Yes.'

My platoon would be more help, Catto was thinking. Move in and move out fast, like with the apples that time, and across the river and the boy is free.

But he knew that was impossible.

Willich said, 'Yes. Write it out. Give it to Gaither.'

Stallo drew a wooden chair to the desk and busied himself with pen and paper.

'There's something else you can do,' Catto said. 'You can delay this execution until you have an answer. This is an appeal. This is the only appeal the boy will have, and Hooker is away and you're in command.'

'A reasonable delay,' Willich said.

'Reasonable!' Catto said. 'I don't see why. Nothing else about this is reasonable. And remember all that about mankind and revolution.'

'Yes, yes.'

'General,' Catto begged, 'could I have some schnapps?'

Catto learned later, with some bitterness, that while he had been forbidden the boy's room, reporters were more privileged. 'I had to,' Willich said. 'I have spent my life fighting the censorship, but if the story had been printed that day a mob of ghouls would have flocked to us. So I asked the publishers to withhold the story for a day. In return I admitted reporters. Do you see?'

Catto saw. By then the fight was gone out of him. When the man from the *Cincinnati Times* arrived, Father Garesche was reading Scripture to Thomas Martin; the two were seated on the boy's bunk, which was carefully made up, as if it might be used again. Martin wore a ball and chain, and a crucifix lay beside him. A fire 'snapped and crackled in the genial old-fashioned fire-place. Near the bunk was hung the scanty wardrobe of the condemned and beneath was a brown jug of water.' Martin was unsure of his age. The reporter thought him under twenty. The boy was unnaturally calm, and asserted his innocence. The *Gazette*, the *Commercial* and the *Enquirer* were also privileged to meet him. The reporters admired him. He was serene and courageous. While they took notes a roly-poly gentleman of cheerful aspect came in to Martin and took his measure. The boy expressed curiosity, and learned that the man was a carpenter, and that the measurement was for a coffin. The reporter from the *Gazette* considered this cruel. Martin remained calm. Father Garesche remained calm. The reporters remained calm. The carpenter achieved his task and left.

Willich, Stallo, Dickson and Catto did not remain calm. They paced. They sent messengers to the telegraph office. Catto chewed at expensive cigars and damned his country in silence. Stallo's telegram had been dispatched. They were all tortured by the passage of horses outside Willich's windows. Each return of the messenger was a moment of hope and grief. Catto thought of his few friends. He would unquestionably leave the army, perhaps the country. Routledge! Routledge had been right! That fat, stumbling, incompetent genius!

By mid-morning the watchers had settled into hopeless silence, and when the messenger knocked and strode into the room Catto scarcely stirred. 'By heaven,' Willich said, 'it's from Hooker!' And they sprang up, Catto agog and then enraged, deriving early knowledge from the messenger's glum mouth and downcast eyes. He sank back into his leather chair. After a pause Willich said in infinite dejection, 'He will do nothing. He says there is nothing he can do. He cannot countermand an order from Washington.'

A new silence fell, a new dimension of horror infusing the oppressive air. 'He could,' Catto said. 'Any other general. Any other general.'

'Catto.' But there was little heart in Willich's rebuke.

'There is still time,' Stallo said; and to the messenger, 'You may go. Be quick if there is news.'

The messenger saluted and went away.

'General Hooker will be leaving this department soon,' Dickson said. 'What a difference a week or two might make!'

Stallo was even more mournful: 'There will be an amnesty. We all know it.'

'The Johnny officers are being wined and dined in every Union garrison,' Catto said. 'Their soldiers are paroled and gone home.'

At noon there had been no word.

'We sat there,' Catto told Phelan later, 'me and Booth and that general with one withered arm and those first-class judges. All that aristocracy and they couldn't do a thing. I kept thinking there was something I could say that would change it all, some magic word, if I could only find it, if only I was a lawyer or a deep thinker. But what? All I could tell them was that men don't kill boys. It turned out they knew that. So there was nothing I could tell them that they didn't already know. Unless maybe that if something this wrong could happen, then maybe there was something wrong from top to bottom. But try telling that to judges and generals. "What what what," they would say. "Anarchy. Anarchy." '

'And what happened?'

'Nothing. We sat about like people with no arms and no legs. I still say Willich could have let the boy go. Sent him across the river and made up a good story about his escape. I'd have taken the blame myself.'

'Not Willich. Willich is a man of honour. A good man, and ninety-nine times out of a hundred you thank God for such men. And the hundredth time is all the more bitter.'

'Honour. He promised me once that nothing would happen to the boy.'

'And who are you beside the government of the United States?'

'I wonder,' Catto said.

'I cannot wait longer,' Willich said. 'An hour after the time already.'

Dickson sighed and Stallo frowned.

Willich asked, 'Where do we stand, Booth?'

'The boy and the priest are ready,' Booth reported. 'The provost marshal will lead. Then the troops, muskets slung, butts up. A closed carriage for the boy and the priest. A hearse following with the coffin. Then the surgeon. I'll be in command,' and briefly his gaze met Catto's, 'but Lieutenant Prentice will command the firing party.'

'Prentice. I thought he was gone.'

'Day after tomorrow, General.'

'His last command.'

'It won't matter.' Booth said. 'He's a dumb roughneck.'

'Yes,' said Willich, 'and we are clever gentlemen.'

'Will you go?' Dickson asked him.

'No. No, I will not. Catto?'

'Yes. I have to.'

Willich nodded. 'Now. That Sands is at the telegraph office, with a fast horse. Silliman is with him. If word comes there will be no time wasted.'

'Silliman? Silliman knows? Silliman is part of this?'

'Yes. He feels as we all do.'

'You could have left him out of it,' Catto said. 'The surgeon is Phelan?'

'Yes.'

'I'll ride behind,' Catto said. He looked at their faces. 'I suppose you're going to tell me this is life, or *c'est la guerre.*'

'No, Catto,' Stallo said. 'It is not life, and the war is over. It is cruel, it is wrong, and it is happening by law in an exhausted republic.'

'The beloved republic,' Willich said softly.

They stood with nothing more to say, as if in a last moment of prayer, as if they were about to part forever.

'It is time,' Willich said. 'God forgive us.'

'If he does, he isn't worth a damn,' Catto said. 'Booth, have you got a horse for me?'

The clouds had thickened, merged, turned grey, and a breeze harried the procession. Catto mounted and fell in beside Phelan, who was subdued and owlish and asked, 'Where have you been?'

'In there,' Catto said, 'and I'll not talk about it now. Just shut your gob.'

'I got an order an hour ago. I'd heard nothing.'

'Have you seen Jacob?'

'No. My God, man, my God.'

'Ah, be quiet,' Catto said.

Strollers stared and murmured, all the way to Mount Auburn, and some ragtag and bobtail followed; Catto turned once to curse them. There was no sign of Jacob.

It was two miles to the execution ground. Towards the end of the march Phelan said, 'The bloody war.'

'Yes.'

But it was not the bloody war and they knew it.

'A little conscientious drinking afterwards,' Phelan said.

'It won't help,' said Catto, and there was the ravine. They had come up a long, winding, uneven trail, tricky for the horses even at a walk. They debouched into the ravine; it was squarish, a hundred feet or so wide. One wall of it was a bluff, almost perpendicular, some twenty feet high, and the soldiers drew Thomas Martin's coffin from the hearse and placed it about twenty-five feet from the face. The boy would be blindfolded and would stand directly before the coffin, his back to the bluff.

Eight men would face him with loaded rifles, one cartridge a blank. Prentice would load the rifles and pronounce the three words. Prentice was a dumb roughneck.

The boy and the priest stepped down, Garesche murmuring. The boy was pale but in command of himself. He stared straight before him and did not see Catto. There was no sun to warm his last moments.

Booth issued orders, stationed the men and conversed with Prentice.

'What do you do?' Catto asked. 'Pronounce him dead?'

'Yes.' Phelan too was pale. 'Will you speak to him?'

'No. What would I say? You speak to him. Tell him all about heaven. How he will be at God's right hand. With the angels and all. And the Virgin Mary baking up a batch of corn bread for him. He's having the last rites and every prayer and attention that money can buy, or the might and majesty of the United States of America.' Catto's eyes brimmed. 'And he will shortly be circling above us on wings of purest white, garbed in a silken bedsheet. Go on. Tell him.'

'God forgive you,' Phelan said. 'He will be in heaven this night. the boy will. Never talk to me like that again.'

'Ah, for God's sake,' Catto said. 'There can't be a heaven! If there's a heaven what the hell's the sense of living?'

Booth inspected the muskets. Behind Catto a murmur: twenty or thirty spectators. He did not see Jacob among them. He damned them again, then stared off beyond them for the horseman who would not come.

Booth led the boy to the open coffin and shook out a blindfold. He seemed to take forever and Catto realized that he was delaying, stretching every motion and word: gazing beyond the crowd. listening. Catto examined them once more. What were they? Shopkeepers? Wives and mothers? He saw a child. a boy of six or seven. The undertaker sat respectfully, his face carefully dismal. on the cab of the hearse.

I should pray. Catto said to himself. For what it's worth. Who knows? Be good to him. God. Forgive him. Don't forgive us.

When there remained no more shilly and no more shally Booth retired towards Catto and signalled to Prentice. Prentice called to Father Garesche, who blessed the boy one last time, placed a gentle hand upon his fair hair, and moved away.

Prentice stood beside his squad, a dark, thick-set man with a full, fanning black beard. Even he, even the dumb roughneck, seemed at a loss: how to begin? He stood for a moment scratching the back of his neck. The mob was silent. Catto fought nausea. Phelan closed his eyes. The undertaker removed his silk hat.

If Catto had not been present he would have believed none of this: not the tragic possibility, not the sickening reality, surely not the mock-heroic climax. The firing party was awaiting its orders, and the crowd stood dead silent before an enormity, even those who approved or enjoyed, standing there some of them holding their breath. This last pause seemed interminable. It dragged on. The crowd murmured, fell silent again.

And then they heard hoofbeats. They heard hoofbeats, and they all turned, all but Thomas Martin, who was facing that way to start with, though blindfolded, and the hoofbeats grew louder, and a man named Lawrence Sands, on a foaming horse, came crashing through the brush, panting and whooping and waving a telegram.

The telegram was signed by Edwin M. Stanton, Secretary of War of these United States, and it said: 'Suspend the execution of Thomas Martin, who was to be executed today, until further orders. By order of the President.'

The reporter for the *Gazette* wrote that the officers looked blank and the soldiers looked curious, 'as they about-faced and marched down the hill again. The crowd, though evidently disappointed, manifested no uncivil or ferocious feelings . . . The undertaker, we thought, seemed to occupy the most unpleasant position, as he drove back with a second-hand coffin to dispose of.'

The *Enquirer*'s man demurred: 'We never saw so happy a set of men in our lives as these soldiers . . . Too much commendation cannot be bestowed upon President Johnson for his promptitude in thus, at the outset of his career, imitating the humane example of his illustrious predecessor, in putting his veto upon the shedding of any more blood; while to General Willich . . . and all the military officers having charge of this execution, there is just praise and gratitude for staying the tragic scene until the very last minute and using the utmost diligence in preventing the effusion of blood.'

And Catto? When they were all gone back down the hill Catto was still there, with Phelan, and he dismounted and sat heavily upon the grassy earth and bawled like a lamb.

Chapter Eight

Out of war. Captain Catto fussed with odds. fumed with ends. This cleaning up. he informed Phelan. was woman's work: tidying a number of privates and corporals. wiping their noses, pinning their nappies and sending them home to mama. 'Peace, peace. All those generals are storekeepers to start with, but this sort of book-keeping and inventory is not for me.'

'You mean you'd like to get back to killing.'

'Why yes. And I suppose you feel the same.'

'Go to hell. I plan to settle in Chicago and become the world's foremost baby doctor. A million red-cheeked Americans scampering back to the nuptial couch and unoriginal sin. I will see to it that their creations survive. The maieutic function.'

'Don't talk dirty.'

'That was a Greek one,' Phelan said comfortably. 'I will minister to these viviparous drudges through term, swab the puling infant and slap it into voice, and guarantee one year of life or your money back. All for six bits. Think of it. Six bits times a million or two. I will do yours gratis.'

'Not for a while, old friend. Any little Cattos will be born into a house and not a tent. And I have my hands full now with other folks' children.'

'The rude and licentious soldiery.' Phelan yawned. stretched, blinked. 'After which you will go on to high deeds as a killer of redskins, is that it?'

'Now, now. After all, it is what I have been taught to do.' Catto executed a knee-bend, flapped his arms, breathed deeply. 'The army held us together in a time of peril and so on. An honourable profession. Also the grub is always there, and the finest of medical attention, and there is plenty of company, and

138

a pretty blue suit, and a country worth having is a country worth warding.'

'Hear, hear.'

'And as for killing . . . ' Catto dropped to a chair and rubbed his thighs. 'This is hard to say. But if I must tell the truth then I tell you there was a moment each time when I loved it. I put a ball through a man's body, and in principle that was wrong but at the time – ah, God.' With a dismayed, embarrassed cluck he added, 'That's pretty awful, I know.'

'Yes,' Phelan said. 'We are a pretty awful species. I won't remind you of the perfections we ought to be imitating.'

'Thanks for that.'

'I will even go further.' Phelan tilted his chair back, smoothed his moustache, and sniffed loudly. 'I have my moments too. When I have a man under the knife, every so often I think how odd it is that I could kill him instanter if I cared to, and no one the wiser.'

'But you never do.'

'Never. I was only trying to show you that we are all full of fell impulse and deadly wish. I once knew the desire to scar Silliman because his face is beautiful and his skin is like a peach.'

Catto said, 'I learn something new every day, and sometimes it's as if I'd always known it.'

Still the men hung about. The ponderous machinery of demobilization creaked, broke down, creaked again. Catto grew tired of the same questions and avoided his troops – save Haller, who fretted only about his lost stripes and his next post. The two of them walked the city, and on Wednesday – May 10th, an important date in Catto's life – they betook themselves to McLean Barracks on a double errand: they would say hello to the boy, and Catto would confer with General Willich on matters of military importance – to wit, Catto's future rank. His commission was temporary, and he fretted. 'You won't make it,' Haller said. 'You're brevet all the way. They'll cut you down to sergeant.'

'Then they can't have me,' Catto said briskly. 'The pistol is at their head, not mine. Phelan says I can make a fortune on the outside. Silliman pleads with me to be a millionaire. Anyway, Hooker likes me.'

'I wish you luck. They may let you keep your epaulets and then hand you a bad assignment.'

'Like what?'

'Some Indian war in the cold country.'

'Won't be cold for another six months. I'll worry about it then.'

'Fair enough. You just get me my stripes back. Nothing brevet about them.'

'Damn,' Catto said, and at Haller's look went on, 'that fat fellow there. Did you see him?'

'No.'

'Reminded me of Routledge. Today's the last day of the amnesty.'

'Sooner or later they'll amnesty everybody.'

'I hope so. That poor fat fool.'

They walked on in silence beneath a clouding sky. Cincinnati bustled gently, shops, wagons, barrels, work gangs, elegant ladies crowding on sail. Catto thought of the boy who had shot him so long ago and how little it meant now; of Sands pounding into the ravine – what if his horse had pulled up lame a mile short! – and Phelan on the ride home from Deer Creek Valley, nervous, relieved, his tongue wagging: 'You see, Marius. Man proposes, God disposes. There is some strange and lovely force at work. The Union wins, which is right and just. The killing is at an end, and your passenger pigeons are back, and the dogwood has flowered again. Redemption and resurrection.' Catto had kept silence, overwhelmed, rejoicing in clemency, shaken to his soul that the army, his army, had survived a peril greater by far than war; rejoicing not only in clemency but also in the luck that had placed him in that ravine at that moment.

He and Haller entered the barracks ceremoniously. General Willich was occupied but would be theirs in half an hour. Captain Booth bade them welcome and led them to Thomas Martin's room, while Catto complained that the young fellow ought to be let loose. 'We can't,' Booth said. 'It was a reprieve, not a pardon. The sentence stands. Got to wait for Hooker.'

'And where is that worthy? Tanking up all the way home? Lying under a table somewhere in Indiana?'

'I'll tell him what you said,' Booth suggested. 'He'll be along some time today.'

'Booth, where's the boy's rifle? That Kentucky rifle.'

'I told you once, locked up right here. He'll have it back.'

'Good. I promised him.'

The door swung wide; Thomas Martin chirruped at them. He was sitting Indian-fashion on his bunk, laying out a pack of tattered cards. He swept them into a heap and swung his feet to the floor. 'Lieutenant!'

'Captain,' Catto said sternly. Haller said, 'Hello, boy,' and the boy said, 'Hello, Sergeant.'

'He'll never learn,' Haller said.

'How they treating you?' Catto took a chair. 'No more ball and chain, I see.'

Thomas Martin grimaced. 'I hated that. Like I was a criminal.'

'That's what you are, all right. No, I guess you're not old enough. What are your plans now?'

'Plans.' The boy fell thoughtful and made a kissing sound. 'Well, you'll never guess.' Without waiting for guesses he smiled shyly and told them: 'I'm going to join the army, if they'll have me.'

'Hallelujah!' Catto crowed. 'But if you're not old enough to be a criminal, you're not old enough to be a soldier.'

'I don't know how old I am,' the boy said. 'I could swear I was eighteen. That's all they want.'

'This will be one hell of an army,' Catto said. 'The redskins will fling us back into the sea.'

'Then you'll be staying in?'

'Can't think of anything else to do.'

'Well, I will if you will,' the boy said.

'Why the hell not,' Catto said. 'Maybe the three of us could serve together,' and they were silent until Catto said, 'and we could see the Pacific,' and they all grew dreamy and ambitious, and passed half an hour in talk of California and the Rocky

Mountains and squaws. It seemed to Catto that his life was rounding to an admirable shape.

General Willich approved. 'Hooker and I will recommend jointly that you be permanently commissioned. He should be back today.' The general raised a hand to him, as if in blessing. 'Why don't I swear you in right now?'

'Right now!' Catto was unnerved, and looked to Booth.

'Technically your hitch is up at midnight,' Willich said.

'Midnight!'

Booth smiled, bland and neutral. Catto studied him briefly. Booth was self-assured, graceful, quiet but nothing of the milk-sop about him. He was perhaps too beautifully turned out, but between him and Dunglas there was a great difference: professional and amateur. Professional: the word pleased Catto inordinately. So did Booth, and Catto was immediately puzzled, almost ashamed, as if he had begun so soon to shift his loyalty and love from Phelan. He remembered the boy then, and Haller, and asked, 'What about my assignment?'

Willich wagged a finger almost roguishly. 'Nix, nix. The army can make no promises. I can recommend you for duty in the west, with Hooker's endorsement. But nothing more.'

Catto looked again at Booth, who was still smiling faintly. Catto grinned at him and said, 'Well, hell, why not? What do I say, and where do I sign?'

Booth's smile broadened, and he winked.

Later Catto joined his civilian friends. 'Gentlemen, I have gone and done it.'

'No.' That odd melancholy crossed Phelan's face.

'Fact. I was carried away. And the general went all patriotic and solemn and I really couldn't disappoint the man, so there I was with my right hand up, and Booth standing there like my best man, and I signed the papers.'

They meditated this heroism.

Silliman said, 'Rank?'

'He thought that between him and Hooker they could keep the straps for me.'

'Second lieutenant. Like me.'

'Like you, hell. You're a dirty civilian at heart.'

'This is a holy hour,' Phelan said. 'A time to give thanks. The world reverting to its natural serenity. We are all alive, Catto has swindled the government out of a commission and Silliman can go home and run for president.'

'That reminds me, Ned. He said you'd be out by the twentieth.'

'This is also unbearably sad,' Phelan said. 'I suppose surgeons will have to stay in until the last gleet is cleared up.'

'Time for a drink,' Catto said. The realization was striking him and he was a bit frightened.

'When is it not,' Phelan said, and dropped a heavy hand to Catto's shoulder.

'You pay, Jack,' said Catto. 'Peace makes all men equal.'

After supper he lay on his bunk studying a map of the western territories. He was at rest: older, thoughtful, settled, inviting repose. He would write again to Charlotte. Now the southwest fascinated him. He must lay in a few boxes of better cigars. He must see about attaching Haller to his future, and the boy if possible; a wry end to a tale of war. The desert, even the mountains, would be a happy contrast to these years of rainy bivouacs, muddy roads, rubbishy towns. He was almost asleep, the map fallen to his chest, when knocking roused him. 'Come in,' he called.

This time it failed him, that sixth sense, that starry instinct; at this exotic social call there was no premonitory nudge, and when he saw Jacob's grief he assumed that the poor man had mislaid his silver dollars, or had been choused by a woman. 'Man, man,' he said, 'it can't be that bad.'

Jacob told him.

They were in the darkened street, arm in arm, Catto tugging Jacob along. 'I heard him,' Jacob said. 'I heard him myself.'

'Who was he talking to?'

'That judge.'

'Stallo?'

'The other one.'

'When was it?'

'Before dinner.'

'What did he say?'

'He wroth, and he yell a lot.'

'Wroth.' Yes. Why not wroth. 'I wroth too. Have you seen Thomas?'

'The Cap'n say they ain't lettin nobody in to see Thomas.'

Catto snarled, whimpered, as a wave of rage broke. 'Ah, Jacob,' he said, and was instantly ambushed by one aching sob; tears disgraced him.

'Don't cry now,' Jacob told him. 'This ain't your doing.'

'It's not that. It's just that he, he, he didn't *do* anything except to me; and the army – the army, Jacob, the army, what do they want with him anyway?'

Jacob had no answer. Before the barracks they paused, as if gathering their forces. Catto looked into Jacob's soft brown eyes and thought that he – officer, white man – ought to say something; but what? He set a hand on Jacob's shoulder.

'A disgrace,' Jacob said. 'Dishonour and disgrace to all.'

Catto's tears had dried. He left Jacob sitting under the gas lamp and went in to Willich. He was rendered weak by a sense of repetition. His knock, his voice, his entrance, and there they were: Willich, Stallo, Dickson. No Booth. He closed the door and stood, impassive. No one spoke for many seconds, and the heart went out of him.

At last Willich said, 'I'm afraid we have some bad news.'

'Yes sir.'

'General Hooker returned this afternoon.' Willich paused to realign his inkstand. 'He has ordered – Catto, I have been transferred! I am to rejoin my command near Nashville next week! And now this!' With his good hand he rubbed his eyes.

'Jacob told me,' Catto said, calmly because he had already assimilated the worst. 'I didn't believe him at first.'

'Who is Jacob?'

'A handyman. The boy's black friend. I suppose if you've been a slave you know these things right way. I was ashamed for all of us, as if I was naked in the street. I couldn't think of anything to say to him.'

Willich gestured to Dickson like a teacher calling for a recitation. 'Tell him.'

Dickson was standing at the window, beside Stallo's chair, hand clenched about a lapel. All these men seemed sightless; they stared at furniture, at ghosts. 'It was my purpose,' Dickson said, and cleared his throat, 'to advise General Hooker, on his return, of last week's events; but I first learned of his return, a few hours ago, from Captain Dunglas, who handed me a note from the general requesting my presence at his headquarters. I went to him immediately.'

'Have a drink,' Willich said.

Catto took up the small glass and listened.

'The moment I saw him,' Dickson said, 'I knew that he was under great excitement. He was trying to suppress it, and to some degree succeeding. He did not look me full in the face, but sideways, looking obliquely, now and then casting a furtive glance at me.'

'Like us tonight,' Catto said.

'Like us tonight. He spoke slowly, and said, "Judge Dickson, I was very angry at you on my return and ordered your arrest; but I have reconsidered it, and am now more composed."

'I was shocked. "Why, you surprise me, General," I said. "What is the matter?"

' "Why, sir," he said, "on my return to the city I found that my administration of this department had been interfered with; that Martin, whom I had ordered shot, had not been shot; that Mister Stanton had suspended my order. I immediately telegraphed him, demanding why he interfered. He replied that it was in response to the Gaither telegram – your work. I demanded of him to send me a copy of this telegram, which he did. Oh, yes, sir! I have got it! I know all you did." '

Dickson sighed. 'You know what General Hooker looks like. Florid. Well, he was a brighter red now, and his eyes were fierce, flashing. "Well, General," I said, "was it not all right?"

' "No, sir," he said; "it was not all right. No, sir. Why, sir, when I was in command of the Army of the Potomac, Lincoln would not let me kill a man. Lee killed men every day, and Lee's army was under discipline; and now, sir, Lincoln is dead, and I will kill this man. Yes, sir, I will. The order is given to

10

shoot him tomorrow, and he will be shot, and don't you inter-
fere."

' "Did Stanton order you to shoot him?" I asked.

' "No, sir. He left the matter in my hands, and I demand that
he be shot – and shot he will be." '

Catto took a chair, and sipped at his caraway liquor. He was
saying farewell to the boy. He knew that. Possibly he had died
in his sleep and gone to Hell. Here we are in Hell. His calm
amazed him and saddened him, and he remembered what
Colonel Bardsley had said about laughing when it was the next
fellow.

Dickson went on. ' "Well, General," I said, "this boy was
only a guerrilla. The war – " '

'But he wasn't,' Catto said.

Dickson shrugged. 'He may have been. And there was the
verdict, on paper. "The war," I went on, "is over. He belonged
to Colonel Jessee's command – " '

'Then he wasn't a guerrilla,' Catto said.

'Catto, Catto, be silent. None of that matters to Hooker.'
Dickson paced. ' "He belonged to Colonel Jessee's command,"
I said. "This morning's papers tell us that the government has
given Jessee the same terms given Lee; that he is now in
Louisville, where he has been feasted and fraternized with by
Union officers. Will it not be shocking to shoot one of his
deluded followers here?" '

This man is making a speech, Catto thought. He talks like a
schoolbook. Will it not be shocking? Yes it will be shocking.

Dickson had both hands at his lapels now. ' "It makes no
difference," replied the general. "Louisville is not in my department. I am not responsible for what is done there. I will do my
duty in my own. Yes, sir, I will; and that tomorrow." And then
he dismissed me.'

No one spoke for some time.

'His manner,' Dickson said, 'as well as his words, told me
that his mind was oppressed with the thought that Lincoln's
humanity had thwarted his career; that if the general had been
permitted to shoot deserters and sleeping sentries when he had
the Army of the Potomac, he would have won the war and

become a national hero, instead of slipping down the ladder to Cincinnati. In some way it is a relief to him to sacrifice this boy.' Dickson bowed his head. 'And not long ago this man held the fate of the whole country in his hands. The Army of the Potomac.'

But Catto was watching Willich. In time Willich looked up and said, 'General Hooker has ordered that the boy be shot tomorrow between noon and two o'clock, and that you command the firing party.'

Catto nodded briskly, as if he had known this for years. He downed his liquor, wiped his mouth and said, 'What will you do?'

'There is no choice,' Stallo said.

But Catto waited, still watching Willich.

'There is no choice,' Willich said.

'I see.'

'I have changed the site. To keep the crowds away. You know the country stone quarry? In Deer Creek Valley but over by that Short Line tunnel.'

'I know it.'

'There is a small field, with a steep hill behind. There.'

'I see.'

'I cannot argue the morality of command,' Willich said. 'I am a general officer and not a private revolutionary. I am probably more horrified by this than you are, because I have seen it before. But I will obey orders. I expect you to do the same. You are a commissioned officer and a professional soldier.'

'Ah, yes,' Catto said.

'Ah, God,' Willich said, his voice at last breaking. 'Here! Here! In Germany, yes, but here!'

'*Alle menschen,*' Catto said, in a foolish tone.

'Hooker!' Dickson said.

Catto thought that the village idiots must feel this way: the frozen grin, the numb mind. 'What happened to Prentice?'

'Prentice has gone home,' Willich said. 'Hooker's orders were specific. He seemed to find some poetic justice in it. It's a bad assignment, Captain. All we can do is get it over with and do

147

better next time. I'm sorry. I can offer no hope. You are to report here at eleven tomorrow morning.'

'No,' Catto said.

They all stared, and he nodded politely. They waited for him to speak, but he had nothing more to say.

Willich asked, 'Do you mean to refuse the order?'

'That's right,' Catto said.

Willich began to speak but stopped himself. Catto knew what the general had been about to say: the whole silly speech, the carrot and the stick, discipline, the greater war won, the small sacrifice, the worm in the rose. He felt again the beat of his own blood, the stretch of air in his lungs, the strength of his heavy thighs. He felt life. That was funny, was it not.

He rose, set the glass on Willich's desk, and stood to attention.

Outside, he threw an arm around Jacob's shoulder. 'You were right.'

Jacob wept.

Catto looked up at the gas lamps, at the faint stars.

'You can't do nothin?'

'I can't do nothin,' Catto said. 'Not only that, my friend, but I am under arrest and confined to quarters.'

'They arrest you,' Jacob said quietly.

Catto nodded.

'They crazy,' Jacob said. 'They crazy men.'

Catto nodded again.

'All they have to do is not kill kill him,' Jacob said. 'That's all they have to do.'

Catto nodded yet again.

Phelan came to him next morning, haggard and deranged. 'My God, boy, I just heard! I just got my orders! Dear Jesus!'

'Have a mug of coffee,' Catto said. 'They treat prisoners well here. Come in, come in. Sit down. I believe it's against regulations but we can always say I needed a maggot.'

'I can't believe this.'

'Fighting Joe Hooker,' Catto said. 'Wants to be remembered for good hospitals, I think you said.'

Phelan sat on the bed. 'I am struck dumb.'

Catto snorted. 'What are your orders?'

'To go out there and declare the boy dead.'

'Nothing to it.'

'Hooker is demented.'

'He is made in the image of God,' Catto said in courteous and reasonable tones. 'I don't believe he's demented at all. He's only human. This has all happened before. In Germany. I have that on good authority. And I've seen boys still younger shot through the belly or the eye or their limbs off.'

'Stop that.'

'All right.'

'How can you sit there like that? Can't we do something?'

'I'm under arrest,' Catto said. 'What would you suggest?'

'They'll break you down to private or worse,' Phelan said, 'and it won't help the boy.'

'I don't give a god damn what they do,' Catto said.

'Ah, you're too pure for it. Is that it? Let them dirty their hands, but not Catto. Is that it?'

'No, no.' Catto spoke gently. 'It's just not my line of work, that's all. Though you've got a point there, about purity. Once they lie to you, there isn't much sense in talking to them again.'

'It can't be just that. There must be some purpose in this.' Phelan was begging. 'There must be. There'll be hell to pay when the story gets out.'

'Nonsense. It will be burked. And then what's one boy more or less? Besides,' he burst out suddenly, 'they shouldn't even be told about it. Let them go on believing and raising their children and saluting the damn flag.'

Phelan said stubbornly, 'Nothing is without a reason.'

'Now listen,' Catto said softly, remembering fifty bushels of Albemarle pippins. 'The last victim of the great rebellion is about to die, and what I've learned today – it was like a vision from on high – is that there will always be a Thomas Martin. It has nothing to do with truth or justice or any of those pretties. If no Thomas Martin is available, then they will go out of their way to find one, or to make one up. So none of your silly comforts. You know better.'

'God help you,' Phelan said. 'God help Silliman too. He's vomiting.'

'Silliman?'

'They've put him in charge of the party.'

'Dear Ned,' Catto said. He stepped to the window.

'Dear innocent Ned. The hope of the future. It's raining.'

'Yes. It's raining.'

'How's Thomas? Have you heard?'

'Booth says he slept badly but ate a big breakfast. He's calm.'

'Yes. He hasn't much to be excited about. Damn,' Catto said. 'Silliman. I wish you hadn't come here with your gossip.'

'Then I'll go,' Phelan said. 'You're as mad as the rest of them. I don't know why I bother to heal anybody.'

'We must talk about that soon,' Catto said. 'Come around tonight, and bring a bottle.'

'Yes. The wake.'

'The wake.' Standing in the doorway he found a weary eloquence: 'Do you know, Jack, I believe you must be right: there is a God. Man alone could not contrive this evil.'

'Be quiet, Marius,' Phelan muttered. 'Watch your tongue.'

'Ah, go along,' Catto said, and turned away, and heard the surgeon's fading footsteps.

He went to the window and looked out at nothing: a street, a city, the feeble rain. After a time he sat on his bed and trimmed a cigar, set a match to it, contemplated swirls of lazy smoke. He lay down, and wondered what was the use of anything. He tried to imagine death. It was unimaginable.

At last he rose, snubbed the cigar, donned his blouse, buckled his belt, inspected his buttons and shoulder straps, hung his sword properly and took up his hat. He walked to the main hallway, where he found Haller. 'Fetch me a horse,' Catto said.

'You're under arrest.'

'Let it be on my head. Fetch me a horse.'

Haller hesitated, but then nodded and left him. Catto waited. After a time he stepped outside and stood beneath the modest portico. Haller rode up, dismounted and held the reins as Catto swung to the saddle. 'The leathers.' Haller looped them over the horse's head into Catto's waiting hands.

Haller said, 'You have to.'

'I have to,' Catto said. 'Silliman couldn't live with it.'

On the cobbles he held his horse to a walk. Traffic was light. Soon he was away from the heart of the city and in a neighbourhood of genteel shops. Hotels. A crew of roadmenders desisted and watched him pass by. He felt their envy. His eyes perceived, registered: the road, the city, a darting cat, umbrellas; his mind refrained from comment (DELAINE 50c YD. LADIES GLOVES 55C) as some of his past dropped away from him for good, no more fun with Phelan, farewell Isaac M. Trout (SHOES $1 AND UP), only this road out of town and the steady rain. Free of pavement, he urged his horse to a gallop. No more what was I, no more what will I be; how could it matter? Fields of honour became swamps of shame even as you trod them.

He slowed to a trot and veered off towards the quarry. At the field he saw them all: the officers together on horseback; the firing party waiting; Silliman pacing; the boy before his coffin, blindfolded; Father Garesche murmuring and gesticulating; the undertaker and his carriage; the spectators; and the rain washing them all clean of colour. Grey, black, hushed, they stood. They all turned towards him, and he saw them as animals, brutes, carnivores. The moment was a flensing: layers of moral blubber, of fatty hope, of sentimental lard were stripped hot from his bones. He pulled up and stared contemptuously at the crowd.

Hoofbeats: Dunglas trotted towards him.

'Go back.' Catto said.

Dunglas reined in. 'A message?'

'No message. Go back.'

'You've broken arrest.'

Catto said nothing. Dunglas trotted back to his station. Catto walked his horse forward, towards Silliman. He searched the crowd and found Jacob, pleading; Catto shook his head and Jacob slumped in disbelief, anguish, despair. Catto wondered if he understood. It would be a small consolation if he understood.

'Marius.' Silliman was drained white, and not so pretty today. 'Are they loaded?'

'They're ready. I was nerving myself.'

'Then get away,' Catto said.

Silliman stood perplexed.

'Get away,' Catto said. 'Go over there with Phelan.'

Rain streamed off Silliman's face. Catto squinted up at a leaden sky. Phelan had started forward and Catto waved him off impatiently.

'You can't,' Silliman muttered.

'Of course I can,' Catto said. 'Do you want me to be formal about it? Lieutenant Silliman, you will join Surgeon Phelan immediately.'

'No. I have my orders. You don't have to do this, Marius.'

'Booth,' Catto called. Booth spurred forward. 'Lieutenant Silliman is under arrest. Please take him in charge.'

Booth growled, 'Come on, Silliman. Get out of it now.'

Silliman was ready for a good cry, and struggled with himself.

Catto dismounted. 'Take my horse, Lieutenant.' Silliman accepted the reins. Thomas Martin was waiting there to be killed. Now Phelan joined them.

'What are you about?' the surgeon demanded in a schoolmaster's tone, leaning down to grip Catto's shoulder.

Catto shook him off. 'I know what I'm about. Keep your hands off me. I've learned something, I have,' he said furiously, his words exploding through the drizzle. 'All on a sudden it's come down to me, what we are and what we're up to, this whole race of pigs, and never mind your god damn God.' Phelan took his horse a step backwards, retreating from this hot assault as if he were a boy private and Catto a foam-flecked colonel. Silliman stood huddled, clutching the hilt of his sword with both hands. Catto pushed by him and marched to Godwinson, marched to him and jostled him backwards with one stride too many; Godwinson too retreated, stumbled, caught himself. 'All right, Sergeant,' Catto said. 'I'm in command.' He wiped his moist hands on his jacket.

'Hooker – '

'To hell with Hooker. Don't you give me trouble now, Godwinson,' his voice rose, the rage returning, 'or I'll bust you down and stand you on a barrel for a week.'

Godwinson said, 'Yes sir.' Beyond Godwinson he could see Thomas Martin.

'Git on with it,' someone shouted. 'The boy's gittin wet.' The crowd murmured, swayed. Mostly men, Catto saw. A few small boys and a couple of women. Hats and caps and cloaks and shawls. Their eyes, hooded in the rain.

'I'd like to be shooting them instead,' Catto said. Phelan had returned to his place, and Booth was leading Silliman off. Catto saw Dunglas again, the cold eyes, the plumed hat. Dunglas hated him. Or he hated Dunglas. But there was no one, at this moment, whom he did not hate. He hated the crow Garesche. He hated Thomas Martin; Hooker; Lincoln who had not acted and Johnson who had; Phelan who gibbered and healed, but not every ailment; Silliman who must be pampered. Catto sought Jacob's eyes, but was denied them and knew that Jacob had not understood. He did not hate himself. He knew what he was doing, and knew that more than most men he had fashioned his own destiny, and that he might someday fashion another destiny, but not soon. He hawked and spat, on all of them.

Garesche had moved off. Catto called out 'Ready!' He wondered if Thomas knew his voice. Of course he did. But the boy stood quite still, soaked, his blond hair plastered flat. Catto looked once more for Jacob; their eyes met briefly and for a moment Catto hoped again; it seemed to him now that only pain was wisdom, and of them all in that ravine probably Jacob knew pain best, but Jacob's eyes said nothing of that, only poured upon him a look of molten accusation. Catto turned back to the boy. Quick. Out of his misery. 'Aim!' Catto bowed his head; a runnel of rain splashed from his hat to his feet, and he raised his head abruptly and with no warning heard himself cry out, 'Thomas! Thomas! You'll be in heaven tonight! Remember that! You'll be in heaven tonight!' He thought, hoped, that the boy's chin rose a fraction, and then Catto said 'Fire.' The rifles roared and Thomas Martin fell backwards into the coffin. The edge of it caught him beneath the knees, so that his feet dangled.

Catto said to Godwinson, 'Take over,' and trudged through

the rain towards his horse. He stood with Booth, Dunglas and Silliman while Phelan examined the boy. Then Phelan came to them and said, 'Major Phelan presents his respects to General Hooker and reports that the prisoner is indeed dead and will not rise again until Judgement Day, when the General will surely meet him again and I hope I am present.'

But Dunglas only said, 'Thank you, Major.' And to Catto: 'Thank you, Captain. That couldn't have been easy, but I'm sure you're back in General Hooker's good graces.'

Catto contemplated this popinjay. There was absolutely nothing worth saying to such a man. But Dunglas was wheeling to ride off.

'Damn that man,' Phelan said. 'Damn us all.'

A hand squeezed at Catto's arm; it was Father Garesche. 'I must thank you,' the priest said. 'It was so good of you, what you said to him. That poor boy – '

'Go to hell,' Catto said, and to Phelan and Silliman, 'Let's get away from this place.' As he mounted he caught a glimpse of the priest's outrage, of the toiling undertaker, of the dispersing crowd.

Halfway back to town Silliman said, 'Oh my God, Marius, I am nothing. Nothing!'

'We are none of us much,' said Catto.

Chapter Nine

And the epilogue: Thomas Martin, who was real, who lived and died as here recorded, lies mouldering in his grave, somewhere in or around Cincinnati. He went to his death 'dressed in light pants, satinet vest, black frock coat, white shirt with no collar, and around his neck a small black string constituted his necktie. On his feet were a pair of rough brogan. He wore on his head a light slouch hat.' He had even slept four hours the night before. He told Father Garesche that he felt he would really die this time. 'He bid good-bye to the officers of the barracks, thanking them for the many kindnesses they had extended to him.' And ' . . . as he crossed the sidewalk towards the carriage in company with Father Garesche he glanced his eye towards the hearse in the rear of the carriage, in which was his coffin, of plain manufacture. Martin smiled and nodded to the undertaker.' He bore himself well on that second journey. As they approached the final field 'his nature mellowed at the spectacle, and he wept for a few moments. Some stimulants were given him and he again rallied.' Captain Booth asked him if he had anything to say in his last hour on earth. Martin said, 'I have nothing to say.' Following military custom the members of the firing squad bore the coffin on their rifles to the waiting hearse.

On May 29th, when Thomas Martin had been dead for eighteen days, President Johnson decreed a full amnesty for all former Johnnys.

Jacob, who was fictional, disappeared into Bucktown and paid no further attention to white men except as necessary to avoid, placate or dupe them. He was a good carpenter and in time became a casual sort of building contractor. He did marry;

he did raise a family. He and they were steady and pious. He never drank at all until late in life, when his travail diminished and he had grandchildren to care for him, and a little nip now and then helped him through the winter. He liked to sit on his porch with a glass of whisky warming in his hand, and tell his friends about Thomas Martin. When he spoke of Catto he spat.

General Joseph 'Fighting Joe' Hooker, who was real, married Miss Groesbeck and retired to Garden City, Long Island, where he died in 1879, sixty-five and garrulous. His life, like his wars, had been full of incident and glory, and upon reflection he found no one event less interesting or important than any other, so he rattled on, and was invited to the best homes.

Edward Flagg Silliman, who was fictional, returned to the mill but never ran for Congress. To mark his home-coming a grand ball was held, at which he was observed to be distraught, perhaps less dashing and appreciative than was meet; this was attributed to the horrors of war. Shortly he announced that he intended to continue smoking cigars, and fell to work improving the business: he modified certain machines, instigated reckless expansions, and persuaded his joyful father to persuade the proper authorities to run a spur from the depot to the mill. It is almost unnecessary to add that he replaced, perhaps ousted, his father sooner than that tycoon had expected; at which the elder Silliman fizzed with pride and dragged his tired grey wife to Europe. Ned married at twenty-nine, taking unto himself a bright-eyed, snub-nosed, dimpled and rich local girl, daughter of a man who owned four thousand acres and lived in town. In ten years she was featureless and dowdy. They raised four children.

Ned remembered Thomas Martin but in time dismissed him as one of the accidents of war. He kept making money and joining clubs and interfering with his pastor and his alderman, so that he was soon a very important man, and it seemed to him that much was expected of him, and he was not wrong about that. With each directorship, with each chairmanship, with each charity, with each five pounds, with each deeper shade of gouty red, he altered the story of Thomas Martin imperceptibly, and eventually heard himself making it quite clear that he had refused absolutely to participate in any such barbarous proceedings. Occasionally he thought of tracing Catto through the army, but one thing or another always came up.

Judge William Martin Dickson, who was real, remained one of Cincinnati's first citizens, in which capacity, in the 1880s, he wrote a letter to the editor – what else? how earnest! how futile! the perfectibility of man! Irate Citizen! Pro Bono Publico! – about Thomas Martin, the only words written about the boy for a century. That is a long silence. 'But why revive these harrowing incidents of the war?' Dickson perorated. 'As well ask, why tell the story of the war at all? If it is to be told, let us have the whole. Let the young not be misled: the dread reality has something else than the pomp and circumstance, however glorious. Besides, there will be other wars and more generals. Let these remember that an abuse of power will rise up in judgement against them.' Foolish optimism, in the style of the time, but most would agree that it was worse not to talk back at all. Dickson died in an accident at sixty-two.

Judge Johann B. Stallo, who was also real, became our Minister to Rome and, in his scientific disguise, elaborated aspects of the conservation of energy, said elaborations being of the first importance to later physicists. His residence in Cincinnati, at 2107 Auburn Avenue, is still standing. He died full of years and honours.

Jack Phelan, who was fictional, did indeed go to Chicago, did indeed become a baby doctor. An air of doom, of mysteries, of profound grapplings clung to him; midwifing was perhaps his answer to the ultimate questions. He married Nell. Believing in repentance and redemption, he had no quarrel with her past; knowing men, and the value of gentleness, she had no quarrel with his corrugated face. They early lost track of Charlotte, who went to New York and was swallowed up. The Phelans prospered and multiplied, and the surgeon – to his startled pleasure – grew corpulent. In time he sported a magnificent row of fobs across a grandly convex vest. He corresponded with Catto, remained devout, and died in 1897 of what used to be called an apoplexy. God knows what became of him then.

General August Willich, who was real, b. 19 Nov. 1810, Braunsberg, Prussia, rejoined his command in Nashville and was then ordered to New Orleans, where he conversed with the upper classes in English, German, French and Italian, and sipped a light wine from time to time. In public he stood for temperance, abstinence from tobacco and gambling, and the perfection of humanity through the exercise of reason and self-restraint. He never lived to see his beloved republic – still awaited – but fought for it always, in the pages of *Der Deutsche Republikaner* and by personal example, and in hundreds of speeches to German groups and veterans' organizations. As a brevet major-general with a disabling wound received in action he enjoyed a pension of thirty dollars a month, and in his sixties he moved to St Mary's, Ohio, where he lived in a rooming house, founded a Shakespeare Study Club, and stood on a street corner near his lodgings every morning and afternoon, watching the children walk to and from school, loving the future in them, thinking his own sad thoughts. The Roman governor Gratus in General Lew Wallace's *Ben Hur* is a portrait of him. In 1878 he died in his sleep.

Marius Catto, who was fictional, rode his hitch west (as a sergeant; he declined the commission) bearing a bedroll and Thomas Martin's rifle, horn and pouch, which he swapped for two months' worth of a Shoshone chief's daughter. He managed to stay out of irons and not to kill. In the last year of his tour he was posted to California, and after his discharge he rode down south and took a job with a freight company, an office job, literacy being prized in that time and place, a job that lasted only until he had met, wooed and won a banker's daughter. She had honey-coloured hair and a fine figger, and they lived on the shores of the Pacific and got six children, desisting only when he achieved what should have been a full measure of respectability by becoming, in the best American tradition, a vice-president in his father-in-law's bank.

He did not enjoy his work. He persisted in seeing money as worthless scraps of paper and chunks of metal, and he disliked an occupation and a circle in which jokes about niggers, kikes and greasers (and often, after a furtive look over a fat shoulder, micks) were apparently a necessity. His future was limited also by certain quirks and blasphemies. Except for his own wedding he declined to set foot inside a church; rather, he enjoyed sitting on his front porch Sunday mornings in an undershirt – the vice-president of a bank! – downing a frothy stein of beer while all those respectable citizens who did not curse or daydream betook themselves to divine services. And while he voted in every election from 1868 on, it was always, as he explained vociferously, for the Green-backer, the Vegetarian, the Prohibitionist or some Chicken-Every-Sunday lunatic, because he would not knowingly support any man with the slightest chance of election, any more than he would have a politician or a preacher to dinner.

Just before the onset of true madness Catto was saved: the town built a hospital, and he transformed himself from financial adviser into administrator, leaving the bank in delight and spending the rest of his active days amid the soothing moans of the moribund. He often wore a stethoscope, and was humoured by physicians, and told the interns stories of ancient simples and nostrums. One day he had a note from Nell: Phelan was dead. Catto drank himself unconscious for the first time in thirty years, weeping like a man because he was weary of his loneliness. He mellowed then, and joined a men's club, and sometimes when the whisky was running he told the tale of Thomas Martin. He maintained that life had no meaning but what we brought to it, and he considered himself the last truly free man in a world careering towards universal slavery. He had no time at the end to reflect or repent, and so died intact; he lived to be eighty-two and was killed by the sun while he marched in a Memorial Day parade. At last his war was over.